DOGSPELL

-or-

Sally & Seemore

&

the Meaning of Mushki

DOGSPELL

-or-

Sally & Seemore

&

the Meaning of Mushki

Written and illustrated by

Karin Gustafson

BACKSTROKE BOOKS

Other Books by Karin Gustafson

1 Mississippi
Going on Somewhere
Nose Dive
Nice

ISBN: 0-9819923-7-4
ISBN-13: 978-0-981992372

For Pearl and Marie — all of them.

I.

Seemie:

Mmmmmm....

Sally:

Dear reader. Hi.

This is a story about me and my dog.

You may be saying, 'not another kid and dog story.'

But my dog happens to be the greatest dog in the world. At least in my world.

Which, okay, was pretty small back when this story began.

4

Back then, my world was just me, my mom, and my mom's inventions (except a lot of those weren't small at all).

Take my mom's Automatic Plantwaterer. It reached all the way from the floor in front of the kitchen sink to some plants on a shelf above it. Meaning it was huge — and, like many of Ruby's inventions — weird.

Ruby, by the way, is my mom. In real life, I call her 'Mom,' but Ruby is what everyone else calls her. She got that nickname because of Rube Goldberg, who was famous for coming up with inventions made of old boots, leaky buckets, grandmothers in rocking chairs, even yowling cats (whose tails were stuck under the grandmothers' rocking chairs).

I always used to be glad that Ruby's inventions weren't quite as weird as Rube's. I mean, sure, they used old boots and leaking buckets — but never a yowling cat or rocking grandmother. Then, I learned that Rube Goldberg only drew pictures of his crazy inventions. Unlike my mom, he didn't actually build them.

What Ruby used for the Plantwaterer was an old coat rack, bicycle chain, garden hose, slightly dented coffee pot, and an old broken accordion. Also one of her home-made motors.

"Mom, no!" I said, when she first dragged it into the kitchen.

"It's a plantwaterer, Sal' it's got to go near plants," Ruby said, nodding up to a row of dried-up ferns. "Besides, it recycles old dishwater."

Another important fact about my mom: she believes in recycling. Only in her case, recycling does not just mean taking used bottles and cans to the dump; it means actually re-using stuff, stuff like:

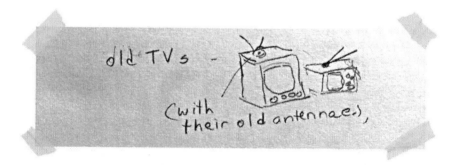

old TVs — (with their old antennae.),

OLD washing machines,

old TIRES,

old computers,

old cords (electrical, bungee, extension, elastic, pants, guitar strings, you name it) —

cords

cords

cords

(old keyboard (plays chords)

"You're going to water plants with old dishwater?"

"Great idea, huh? It'll probably save a gallon or so every day."

Saving is another passion of my mom's, as in, saving the planet.

I looked down at the sink. The suds were dotted with the eggs we'd had for breakfast. There was also a big red smear that I was pretty sure was the hot sauce my mom put on her eggs. (It really got her going, she always said.)

"Won't soap hurt the plants?" I tried.

"Not one little bit," Ruby said.

She carefully tugged the Waterer onto some X's she'd chalked on the floor. The few pearly keys left on the accordion seemed to grin down at me.

"I've got to get it on these spots, see," Ruby said, "so that the water will hit the plants. I plotted it all out with those calculations I had you do for math the other day."

Calculations *I* did?

I stepped further back.

"Ready?" Ruby whispered, reaching for my hand. (Trying out a new machine was always a big deal for her.) She used her other hand to flick a small switch wired onto the Waterer's coat rack.

"Come on come on come on," she whispered.

A whirr began; a big slurping slurp; and *heeeooo* — *haawwooo,* the accordion (still grinning) groaned.

"Is it supposed to sound like that?"

"Pretty cool, huh?! Saves water, saves plants, and even makes music!"

HEEEOooo, groaned the accordion.

"Oh yeah. Cool, mom," I said.

II.

Seemie:

Sniff...ouch...sniff...oooooo....

Sally:

Like many of my mom's inventions, the Automatic

Plantwaterer had a few kinks. One of these showed up a few days after installation when it dropped a spoon on my head.

Ruby said she was really sorry. (*Great.*)

And that fitting a little screen onto the hose would be an important safety feature. (*Now, she thinks of it.*)

And wasn't I lucky it wasn't a fork.

But I didn't feel lucky. I felt pain. I also felt a big red bump on my forehead. (Even though I knew touching it would only make it worse.)

Which was what took us to Scotto's ice cream stand — Ruby wanting to make it up to me — and Scotto's was where we saw the three girls.

It probably seems strange, but, back then, I didn't know much about girls. (Other than myself.)

I didn't know much about boys either.

I didn't know much about kids of any kind. This was because my mom believed that children should be home-schooled until they could build a decent two-stroke motor and a simple radio transistor. (Though I'd managed some good one-way radio transmitters, my motors still tended to clunk out.)

But even with my limited experience of other kids, I could tell (i) that the girls were about my age, and (ii) that they were trying to act a whole lot older. One had long, shiny blonde hair that looked like she brushed it three hundred times a day. The other had braids dyed purple. The thirds had short black hair that hung down like a curtain on one side.

"Is that all?" the blonde girl said.

"We wanted mediums," said Side-bangs.

This was weird. Because Scotto had given them huge ice

cream cones. But the girls made such a fuss that Scotto finally just charged them for baby size. Then the girls, smiling sideways so Scotto couldn't see, balanced their huge cones over to one of Scotto's little park benches.

There — and I know because I sat on the other park bench — the girls made fun of Scotto. He had a nose, they said, like an old ping pong ball.

They also made fun of my mother. (She was up by Scotto's window talking to him — probably about the ice cream machines, which she was always helping to fix.)

In her case, they laughed at her clothes — a mechanic's onesie with the name *Stan* sewed on its front.

Then, they made fun of me. (They were whispering so that I

couldn't actually hear that part, but I could tell from the way the bump on my head hurt.)

I put my hand up to hide the red spot. I tried to act as if I was just brushing the hair out of my eyes — you know, for five minutes straight

Finally, Ruby and I trooped back to the truck.

"Head better?" she asked.

"I guess," I said.

I tried to make my voice sound normal, but I must not have done a good job. Because Ruby turned to me (even as she put the truck into gear) and gave me this searching look she had. It was the kind of look she used on an invention that wouldn't work or a machine that had somehow gone haywire, a look she saved for something that needed to be fixed.

I turned my face out the window.

"Hey, Sal," Ruby said, voice brightening, "you want to go to the playground?"

"No," I said.

"There might be some kids there."

"Mom," I said.

Something about that last 'mom' shut her up for a little bit. But I could tell that that she was still thinking about me, thinking hard.

"There's that old computer out in the garage," she muttered. "Hey, I bet I could fit some arms and legs on, get one of those big dolls...."

"Would it have to be able to walk?" she asked. "Or, could it just sit on your desk?"

"Could *what* sit on my desk?"

"Your new friend."

"Huh?"

"I was thinking I could invent one."

"Mom, you can't *invent* a friend."

"Sure, you can. Well, *I* can. *If* I get all the right materials, and I've probably got most of them stored out back."

"Mom — but it wouldn't be real."

"Sure, it would be real."

"I mean ... it wouldn't ... be *alive*."

Ruby sighed. "I know that, sweetheart. It would be a robot. But it could be the coolest robot in the world — I've got so many old computer parts. Gee, we could even use that blonde wig I found."

"Mom, I don't want a computer with a wig."

I turned my face back out the window.

This time we were quiet for a while, Ruby not even muttering, me just staring out at a world blurred by the truck and also, I admit it, tears. It was a world of greens (yards) swishing into grays (tree trunks), reds (bricks), white (a little wood fence), and then, in a single moment that seemed suddenly clear and bright, a little blue dog house

"Hey Mom, wait a second," I said. "If I can't find a human friend, then maybe I could have, you know ... a pet."

Ruby's body twitched (which was actually kind of scary since she was still driving.) It was as if the robot, humming away in her mind, had just had its plug pulled.

"Sally, be serious," she said.

"I am being serious."

"Sally, come on," she said.

"Mom, I'm serious."

"Do you really think a pet would be better than a robot?"

"Mom!"

III.

Seemie:

Yeoowwww!!!!

(Sniff — oooo — sniff — whimper —)

(Sniff — blub. Sniff — blub. Sniff — blub blub blub

blub.)

Blub?

"Fish do too have personality," my mom said.

Sally:

But fish were just so pretty, Ruby said.

But fish have no personality, I said.

But she could just watch them going back and forth in the fish tank all day long, Ruby said.

But watching fish go back and forth would be like watching a washing machine, I said.

"But you used to like that, Sal, when you were little," Ruby went on. "I used to set up a teeny stool at the little round window of the front-loader."

"Just because I was a weird little kid doesn't mean I have to be

22

a weird big kid," I said, and that anyway it was all her fault.

Finally — finally — Ruby said we could look. "But, just look, mind you."

So, we went to the pet store to 'just look.'

But, secretly, I brought every bit of money I'd saved up, which included one birthday twenty from my grandparents and all the money I'd earned sorting screws, bolts, and other little bits of machinery Ruby stored up for her fix-it and invention business.

But ... sigh.

Maybe the problem was our local pet store. It wasn't a little-dogs-and-cats-in-the-window kind of a pet store. It was a reptiles-fish-mice-birds-and-a-lot-of-fake-castles kind. There were some neat animals, don't get me wrong — iguanas with sideways arms, little blobs of guinea pig, all kinds of beady eyes.

And, oh yeah, fish. ("Just look, Sal," Ruby said.)

But I was just-looking for a friend, and nothing in those wire cages or glass tanks seemed to qualify.

Then I noticed a big cardboard box under a catnip stand. It was a box that quivered, almost seeming to breathe. Stacked in one cardboard corner were three tiny little, round little, pudgy little, breathing little —

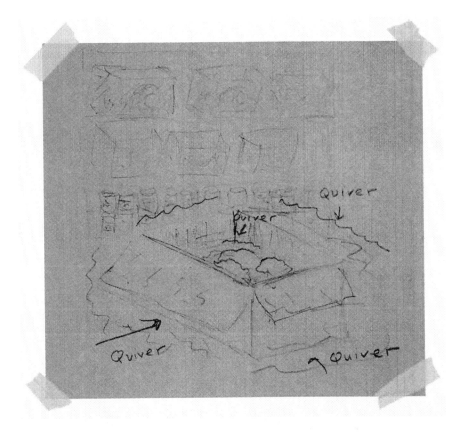

I knelt down.

The littlest squirmed out from under the others and stumbled over to my hand, which it began to lick like crazy, its little pink tongue warm as hot milk.

I carefully lifted the little licking puppy from the box.

"Oh Mom, isn't it just so cute?" I said.

"Awww," Ruby said.

"And see, it likes you." (The puppy, already showing signs of great intelligence, licked Ruby's fingers.)

"Aawww," she said.

"What a sweetheart," the salesman said. "He's cheap, too, because he's not completely purebred. Just the cost of his shots."

"I know we were just coming to look, Mom —" I tried.

And then the little guy — the puppy — just looked. Only, you know, up. At me, at my mom, and "awww," Ruby said....

IV.

Sally:

Our ride home was the happiest day of my life. (Even though it only took about twenty minutes.)

The pup was a mutt, but the salesman said he looked like he was mainly bichon frisé. Bichon frisé means curly dog in French, and they are usually little white dogs, with curly fur, big black eyes, black noses and little black lips. That sounded just like our puppy, only he also had an adorable pale grey splotch over one eye, and one on his side too.

All the way home we tried to come up with names.

Ruby suggested Spot, Frizzy, Goliath, Fenster....

Okay, so, those were wrong.

When we pulled into our driveway, the pup stood on my lap,

peering hard out the window.

"That dog has the most intent gaze I have ever seen," Ruby said. "Look at him, staring, watching, seeing everything ."

"I've got it, Mom! Seemore. Get it? Like See More, because of the way he looks at everything."

"So you'd spell it S-e-e-m-o-r-e rather than S-e-y-m-o-u-r."

"Sure. I mean, I guess so." (Spelling was never my strong point.)

"I think that's great, Sal."

"And we can call him Seemie for short."

The puppy looked up at me. Now, he also seemed to be listening hard.

"Seemore — that's you're name, okay, Seemie?"

Seemie:

See — rrrr — Mee?

V.

Seemie:

Sniff... sniff... mmm....

"Here, Seemie!"

Sniff... mmm ... mmm....

"No no, not there Seemie! Not on Mom's flowers! Here. That's right. Good boy! Oh what a good little mushki! You deserve some CHEESE!"

Sniff... CHEESE???

Sniff chew sniff yum sniff mmm!

CHEESE!!!

Sally:

Aww….

Seemie:

"Seemie — you want to PLAYBALL?"

PLAYBALL not CHEESE, but fit in mouth run run.

"Seemie — let's go OUTSIDE."

OUTSIDE not CHEESE, but grass-stuff, Ruby-stuff,

not-on-Mom's-flowers-stuff. Still sniff good yum yum.

DOGFOOD not CHEESE! Yech! Sniff wait sniff wait

sniff wait.

"Mom, we can't let him starve."

CHEESE!

Sally:

We didn't really understand how smart Seemie was at first.
But we did notice that the little mushki was nutso about cheese.

Seemie:

CHEESE Seemie's first word.

Well, SEE ME Seemie's real first word.

So Seemie know SEE ME and Seemie know CHEESE.

And when Seemie hear them, Seemie sniff listen up good.

"Let's play Pirate," Sally say.

"Grrr," Seemie say, like someone steal my CHEESE.

"Hey, Seemie. You want to play tag? "

See Sally run. See Me run! Maybe CHEESE somewhere!

"Oh Seemie, I love you so much."

LOVE mean: hmmm ... not CHEESE. Yes, CHEESE! Seemie LOVE CHEESE! (Mmm!)

But LOVE also mean SALLY (sniff), TUMTUM (pat), OH YOU LITTLE MUSHKI.

Sometimes Seemie even try talk. When Seemie sniff sniff sniff LASAGNA —

'PLEASE,' Seemie say, and WAVE WAVE WAVE paws.

"Here Seemie, you want a carrot stick," Sally say.

CARROT STICK, NO! That not what Seemie mean!

But paws say only WAVE WAVE WAVE.

It so furrr-rustrating!

Then one day it RAIN so hard that everything just change.

VI.

Sally:

Seemie and I were playing in Ruby's workshop and had just knocked over our fifth pile of recycleables, a mix of flashlight and headlight faces that Ruby said she liked for their tough glass.

"Okay, kids, that's it. Outside," Ruby said.

"But, mom, it's raining outside."

"Oh gee," Ruby sighed, looking out the streaming window. (It was actually pouring, but, when Ruby was in her workshop, she tended not to notice things like that.)

"So," she said, "I guess you need a better place to play *inside.*"

"Yes, and not where we're supposed to work on another motor," I said. "Or a radio transmitter either."

"But you've gotten so good at walkie-talkies, Sal. That teeny

36

one is amazing."

"Thanks, Mom, but this is Saturday —"

"Hey, wait a sec. What about the attic? I should check on leaks anyway, a rain like this."

Seemie:

I always think "A TICK" mean brush fur. But Ruby lead us to very top of house.

"I can't believe I'd almost forgotten it," Ruby sigh.

"A good thing too," Sally whisper, "or otherwise it would be full of old junk."

I sniff. There a lot of stuff here. But not Ruby-stuff. At least not machine-stuff. No CHEESE either. (Darn!)

No, it smell like ... rrr ... wood, paper, and ... rrr ... dust. Some flat dust, some rrr-floaty dust.

"At least, there's no leak," Ruby say.

Sally walk slowly around wood stuff.

"Those shelves hold your Dad's things," Ruby say. "His books." Then Ruby sniff sniff sniff sniff. (Must be all that dust.)

"Daddy's books?" Sally say.

"You knew he was a professor?"

"A college professor, right? I saw that picture of him with the funny robe."

"That was on one of their graduation days. College

professors need to read — or, have read — a whole lot of books."

"Good books?" Sally ask.

"Great books, some of them," Ruby say. "Hey. There's even your dad's old dictionary." Ruby pat BIG book. Then, all sudden, sniff sniff sniff, smell sad.

When Ruby smell sad, I feel bad. So I go to her, paw air. But gently (wave wave wave), so she know it not PLEASE CHEESE I want.

"Aw, Seemie, you need some attention," she say. "Here, let me hold you a little."

(Whoa! Ruby pick me up and toss me onto shoulder.)

"Mom, I have a question. Could I have this place as my play area? For Seemie and me, I mean. I promise we won't hurt anything."

"That's exactly what I was thinking," Ruby say. "How

about we push some of the things against the wall so you have a nice open space?"

"But can we keep the desk out in the middle?"

"Sure."

"And look at this little blackboard! We could use that too, right? And here's some chalk!"

CHALK — sniff. Means white stuff look like CHEESE. But only look. (Darn!)

Soon Sally and Ruby push around wood stuff, books, dust.

"Oh Seemie," Sally say, "a place for just you and me right?" giving me a good good ear scratch scratch —

I lick thanks Sally's cheek.

"Oh, you little mushki," she say.

VII.

Sally:

Life changed for Seemie and me up in the attic. Maybe it was

the desk and the blackboard. Maybe it was spending time with the spirit of my dad, the college professor. All I know is that Seemie and I suddenly had just one game and we played it nearly all the time.

The game was "School."

I was the teacher, and Seemie, the students. All of them. This was a little hard at first, but Seemie soon got the hang of it.

"Good morning, class. And how are you this morning?" I would say every morning in my best teachery voice.

"Rrr," Seemie would say, sitting on a box in the front of our classroom.

"Today, class, we are going to study the letter 'B.'"

"Rrr," Seemie said.

"B stands for boy and, uh, ball, and ... uh," I leaned over the desk to leaf through my father's huge dictionary, "bannister! You know, that thing on the stairs that you slide down."

"Rrrrr — rrrr — rrr."

"Very good, Donald. But next time, raise your paw please — I mean *hand* — if you're going to talk. Does anyone have another 'B' word?"

At this point, I'd usually pick up a yardstick and begin pacing the attic floor. Seemie, for his part, would trot over to another box and, leaning on it, slowly raise a paw.

"Yes, Betty. And what's your B word?"

"Rrrry."

"Berry?"

Seemie shook his head. "RRRRrrryyy. RRrrryyy."

"Ohh, Betty! Your name! Excellent. Wait a minute Bet —

LEONARD!"

The minute I said *that* name, Seemie hopped down from the nice smooth Betty box to an old torn rumpled box and began madly chewing its corner.

"LEONARD!" I shouted, banging my yardstick on the floor. "Stop that right now! How many times have I told you not to mess up your desk?"

Seemie stopped. ("*Good dog, Seemie,*" I whispered.)

"Mmmm," he whimpered back.

"That's okay, Leonard. Just don't do it again."

"Rrrr," Seemie nodded.

I always worried that all of the "good dog/bad Leonard" business would confuse Seemie, so I never made him be Leonard too long. But the truth was that Seemie never seemed very confused by anything.

Which should have been a sign, I guess. That something very

strange was going on in our little game.

And that, pretty soon, it was going to get a whole lot stranger.

VIII.

Seemie:

It hot day in attic. And Seemie hungry.

Still, Seemie try.

"Okay, now, Rupert," Miss Sally say. "The answer to three take away one is...."

Seemie shut eyes. Seemie try to shut ears too. Seemie cannot con-con-concentrrate if he listen for fridge yumming, you know, two floors down.

"Come on, Rupert, you can do it," Miss Sally say. "Three take away one is...."

"Roo," Seemie try.

"Ttttrroo," Seemie try again. "Rrr-Twooo!"

All sudden, Seemie hear clock tick. Attic so quiet.

Seemie open eyes. Sally's eyes open too! Good Sally!

"What did you say, Seemie?" Sally speak now just like regular Sally, not Miss.

Seemie pant once, twice, then "twoo," Seemie say. "Rrr-three take away rrr-one is twooo."

"Tick tick tick," say clock so loud till "ohmigosh!" Sally cry, even louder than clock!

"Seemie, are you talking? Seemie, you're talking! You're talking! Seemie, wait a second, can you really talk?"

"RRR-yes. Seemie rrr-talk. RRR-at reast, Seemie try talk."

"I mean, I'm not just imagining this, am I?" Sally say. . "Wait a second. Is this a dream, Seem?"

"No, Sal. It not rrr-dream-seem, I mean...rrr... dream."

"Oh wow!" Sally hug me.

"Oh wow!" Sally hug me again.

Then she jump. She laugh. She run to staircase. She run down, then up, then down again.

"Mom! Mom!" she call. "Guess what! Seemie can talk. SEEMIE CAN TALK."

"I think she out at rrr-repair call," Seemie say.

"Oh yeah, sure. Oh yeah, I forgot."

Now Sally down on her paws, rrr-hands, and look at Seemie, eye-eye.

"Honestly, Seemie. Can you really talk?"

"Rrr-it okay Sal?"

"Oh Seemie, it's not just okay. It's wonderful!"

Sally:

It was crazy. It was impossible. It was ... fantastic.

My dog, my Seemore, my own little mushki, could talk!

I could hardly believe it — even after Seemie and I spent the next hour at it. (Well, Seemie talking — me freaking out about Seemie talking —)

"Seemie no talk good," he whimpered.

"Seemie, you *do* talk good," I told him. "You talk better than any animal I ever heard of. But look," I said, patting him. (He was getting awfully tired.) "Why don't we just take a little break, huh? How about we go look up talking animals on Mom's computer? Then you can see how great you are."

We went downstairs and Seemie sat on my lap as I searched for talking animals. When the list of videos and websites popped up, "rrr-look Sal, parrrr-rrot!" Seemie said.

"Where?" I asked, looking for a picture.

"Rrr-right here. See, *P... A ... Rrrr ... Rrrrr ... O....*" Seemie pressed his little black nose to the screen, oozing it along each letter.

I gently pulled Seemie's muzzle from the screen, then turned

his little face towards mine. He hated it when I held his face that

way, but I really needed to look straight at him.

"Seemie, this is getting weird. So, now, you can read? I

mean, seriously, are you telling me you can read?"

"Rrr-Seemie don't know," Seemie said, trying to look down.

I let his face go.

"Rrr-I mean, I guess," Seemie whispered, now staring into my lap. "A rrr-ittle."

"Seemie, listen. This is important. How did you learn all this stuff?"

"Rrr-all dogs can't read?"

"No dogs can read! Oh Seemie," I said, hugging the back of his head.

"But *you* teach me, Sal. Remember? A is for rrr-apple; B for...ban-ban-bannister."

"Yes, but, that was just a game." I said, hugging Seemie one more time. "Mom will help us figure it out, I guess. Or if she can't, she'll know how to find someone who can. Some scientist or other." I laughed, then scratched Seemie behind the ear so he would relax a little. After a few scratches, he grinned in this lopsided way he had, all his teeth showing on one side.

"All the scientists will just go crazy about you, Seemie," I said. "You're like an Einstein or something. A dog Einstein."

"What rrr-Einstein?"

"He was this genius guy with really messy hair."

"Is Seemie rrr-hair messy?"

I kissed the tangled curls on his head. "Your fur is terrific. But, hey, let's look at that parrot."

I clicked onto the website. "Look, he only knows about 200 words, and they think he's a big deal."

We jumped from site to site. The videos of dogs were usually dogs howling in a way that just sounded like talking — it wasn't true *conversation.*

Then we came to a site that showed animals in cages. One monkey had a bunch of wires clipped to his head. His eyes looked terrified, and his little monkey lips seemed to cry.

"Sal, what are rrr-experrr-i-ments?" Seemie asked.

"Experiments? It's like when scientists test something. Sort of like ... um ... taking your temperature. "

Seemie began to tremble. Then I remembered how *his* temperature was taken. "But they probably wouldn't do that," I said.

Seemie trembled harder.

"Oh, Seemie, calm down. They'll probably just make you do puzzles and stuff."

"Just rrr-puzzles?"

"Well, they might want to check out your throat a little, because you can talk. And maybe…um…your brain."

Something suddenly shook us like a gong. Only it rang with silence rather than boing. I turned off the computer and carried Seemie up to the attic. He could have climbed up the stairs himself, but I didn't want to let him out of my arms for even a second.

I sat him down on the desk.

"Are dog scientists rrr-nice?" Seemie croaked.

"Sure, they are," I said, patting the entire length of his side. "They're like vets."

"Vets!!!!" he yelped.

Oops.

Seemie:

Rrr-white coats. Cold tables. Long sharp pointy things.

And they always say it not going to hurt.

"I thought rrr-talking good," I say.

"Oh, Seemie, talking IS good," Sally say.

Just then, we hear Ruby downstairs.

Seemie — rrr-me — wiggle, wanting to see her, wanting to say hello. (It a dog thing.) But Sally hold me tight.

"Seemie," she say, "I don't think we should tell Mom about this yet."

"No?"

"It's just that, if she knows you can talk, she'll feel like she has to do something about it."

"Rrr-call dog scientists?"

"I don't know. But maybe we'd better just keep quiet about it a while."

"RRR-uff," Seemie — I mean, *I* say, "I mean rrr-right."

IX.

Sally:

Days passed, weeks, and even though Seemie and I talked nearly all the time, it was still hard for me to believe that he could actually do it.

Oh sure, he sometimes had trouble keeping the bark out of his voice. R's were especially growly. But Seemie was my best friend even when he couldn't talk, and now that he could —

Even though it was summer, we still spent a lot of time up in the attic — it was one place we were sure Ruby couldn't hear us. But we never played school again. No, we mainly just ... talked. I would tell Seemie people things — he especially liked learning the names of stuff — and he would tell me dog things — like how great grass smelled in the early morning (but not, he said, so good as cheddar.)

Sometimes, Seemie would try to tell me his life before the pet store. Except it was hard, he said, to talk about things that happened before he knew words — "real words," he said, meaning, I guess, *human* words; it was hard, he said, to even *remember* things that happened before he knew words.

"It kind of, you know, rrr-blur," Seemie said. "Like fur. Like when I put my head in my paws and the curls so close they clouds."

He put his head in his paws, I guess, to show me. We were in my bed just then, getting ready to go to sleep.

"My mom," Seemie said, shutting his eyes, "was *mmmmmmm*, super *mmmmmm,* except you know, when she'd pick me up — *ouch* — by my neck. That was kind of ... rrr-*yeow!*

"And my brothers and sisters — they had these little round ... rrr ... bellies, and they were pretty *mmmmmmm* too, only their paws were *yeow!* You know, always stepping on me....

"Then," he said, opening his eyes wide, "there were this great big *YEOW!* That was when they took us all away."

"Wow," I whispered. "That must have been terrible."

"Yes," Seemie said, his head pressing into my side. "And that brown rrr-cardboard box. It not *mmmmm* at all."

I actually had fond memories of that brown cardboard box, since it was where I first found Seemie. But I stroked his back now, trying to make up for its non-*mmmmmness*.

"Even with the blubs," Seemie went on.

"The blubs?"

"They the ... a ... a ... quaaaa ... aquaaa...."

"Aquariums?"

"Yeah," Seemie nodded. "The blubs were nice. But in that box, my brother/sister toes as sharp as — what that word, Sal, begin with "c" like cat?"

I thought a second.

"Claws?"

"Their paws like claws." Seemie shivered into my inner arm.

"Yeow," I whispered.

"But you came, Sal — you and Rrrruby —" Seemie raised his head to look right at me. "You picked me up and not even by my neck —"

I patted flat the soft curls at Seemie's neck.

"You a great girl, Sal," Seemie said.

"You too, you little Mushki." I said. "I mean," I laughed, "you're a great dog."

For just an instant, Seemie smiled — that crooked dog grin — then licked his little black lips, then tucked his little head back into my side again.

I knew then exactly what Seemie meant when he talked about feeling *mmmmmmm*.

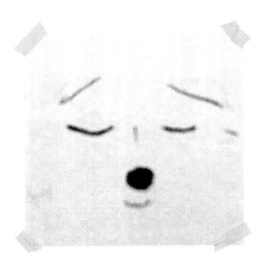

X.

Sally:

But *mmmm* doesn't always last very long.

The next morning, even before the first heehaw of the Automatic Plantwaterer, Ruby stomped into our room.

"Sal," she said, looking at me in that way she had — that is, the way of the fix-it person.

"And a good morning to you too, Mom," I said, determined not to be fixed.

Which Ruby suddenly seemed to get, because "oh ... um, sorry, Sal," she said. "Good morning!!

"And, Sir Seemore — a good morning to you too!" she went on.

Seemie immediately began wriggling.

(That's right, Seemie, distract her, I thought.)

It worked for at least a minute, Ruby patting Seemie and saying, "aw." Then, her face switching back to "fix-it" mode, "I've been thinking, Sal," she said. "Your motors are decent and that teeny walkie-talkie is so darn cool. So...."

"So?"

"So, I think it's finally time for you to start school."

"School?"

"Real school. You know, the one in town."

"Mom, I do go to real school," I said, pressing my hand on Seemie's back. (His little tail was already filling with wag.)

"I read real books, learn real math. Anyway, my motors are terrible."

"Motors aren't the point, Sal," Ruby sighed. "There are things I just can't teach you here at home, things you need to learn from other teachers, other ... kids."

"But, mom," I tried.

"Sal," Ruby said firmly. "It's just too lonely here — no one for you to play with, no one even to talk to."

"But I do have someone to play with," I said, nodding towards

Seemie, who looked up to her meaningfully.

"Aw," Ruby said, patting him. But then she looked back to me (also meaningfully.)

"Seemie's great, Sal," she said. "But he's a dog."

"But, Mom," I tried.

"Sal, it's time," Ruby said. "You always said you wanted to start in the beginning of the school year, right? Well, that is coming up right now."

"But," I tried once more.

"But nothing," Ruby said. "Think of all the equipment, Sal," her eyes brightening now for real. "I just bet you'll learn all kinds of new things too even on the very first day."

Seemie:

Sally and I climb to attic.

"What so bad about real school, Sal?" I ask. (We still on attic stairs, so I practice my soft-speak.)

"Oh Seemie," she sigh. "I'll have to leave you to go to

real school. Leave you every single day."

"Leave rrr-Seemie?"

"Didn't you know? Dogs can't go to real school."

"Not even," I ask, "if they always raise their paws?"

"Not even if they always raise their paws," Sally say.

Then she reach down, pick me up. Not by neck, but by my whole body. So soft. So gentle. Yet, still it feel so yeow!

Only that not really the right word. I don't even know the right word for how yeow I feel.

"Oh, Mushki," she say.

XI.

Sally:

On my first day of school, I learned a lot of new things, just as Ruby predicted.

The first thing I learned was that if you came early, you had to wait outside. Even if it was raining.

The second thing I learned was that umbrellas are usually not made of bits and pieces of material that my mother said looked like a dolphin frolicking in the waves, but actually looked like a blue hot dog getting chopped up in a food processor.

But, I jump ahead.

When Ruby and I first got to school, it was hardly drizzling. We were early, but so were lots of kids, all chatting and laughing.

I tried to look sort of chatty, sort of laughy too. The trouble was that I wasn't actually talking to anyone. I was just so different.

For one thing, they were all shiny. Everything about them seemed new — their clothes, their backpacks, their hair. Even — and yes, I know this sounds weird — their teeth.

I suppose it was possible that I was shiny too, but not a single thing I had was truly new. Sure, Ruby had made some special stuff for me, but it was all constructed out of recycled material (like the backpack she sewed of parachute silk and snakeskin. Parachute silk, she said, to keep it light and strong, snakeskin so it would be rugged.)

At least, my hair was clean, and, luckily, I didn't need braces. (Knowing my mom, they'd probably be made out of used coat hangers.)

All I could think about was going home.

"Do you think, maybe, we should go back to the truck?" I tried, as the drizzle morphed to heavy rain. But my mom just smiled her know-it-all inventor's smile, reached into her bag, and came out with what looked a like a thick wad of colored cloth.

"Cute dolphin, huh?" she said, as the huge blue hot dog bloomed above us.

"I really think, Mom, that the truck would be better."

Just then, a short woman with billowing purple pants and a long black braid scooted up.

"What a monsoon! Can you slip under there, Pradip?" the woman said, edging a skinny, brown-skinned boy towards the school's overhang.

Although the boy looked a little like his mother, he did not look like anyone else. That was because he wore a white shirt, black tie, and grey wool shorts creased down the front, as if they had just been ironed. (Even so, they did not look shiny. Maybe because they were right in the middle of getting soaked.)

"Do you want to share our umbrella?" Ruby asked.

The woman stared up. "You've got room?"

"Sure," Ruby said. Now she pulled at something in the umbrella's webbed roof. "If I bring down this other handle, we can get another few square yards."

As the umbrella's second handle came down, the roof doubled.

"Oh me," the woman exclaimed. "Just look at it."

It was then that I noticed the three girls. (Somehow, I didn't feel like looking up at the second blue hot dog.) I realized then that they were the same three girls who'd been at Scotto's the day I'd been banged by the Plantwaterer, the girls who'd complained about their huge ice cream cones.

Talk about shiny! The blonde girl seemed to have some sparkly stuff on her hair and cheeks and gold earrings bright enough to *ting*.

"Sal," Ruby said. "Pradip here also has Mrs. Burke. And he's new too. They've just moved from India."

"Your mother's umbrella is fantastic," Pradip said, with a toothy smile.

"I guess." I said.

"Are you nervous?" Pradip asked, smile gone. "I am. I hate starting new schools."

"Have you started a lot of them?"

"Only my old one in Delhi. You know, back in pre-primary.

When the school bell blared, even the bricks seemed to jump. Certainly, Pradip and I did. Then the whole world — at least that part of the world that encircled us — began to rumble.

XII

Seemie:

She gone.

And there nothing I can do about it.

There nothing I can do at all.

Except eat, sleep, and rrr-pad around the house.

Sally learning all-new things, and me just eating, sleeping, and rrr-padding.

What the point?

I start to climb — so slow — to attic, even though I still smell half a bagel in my food dish, half a bagel with cream cheese. From Sally, sniff, good Sally.

Okay, so maybe, sniff, I don't climb to attic just yet.

Sally:

As school buses poured kids onto the sidewalk, we were pushed into the building.

I turned to my mom to tell her we just had to go home. *Now.* But it was Pradip next to me, his face grey, maybe even greenish.

The sight of him grey/green somehow made me instantly calmer — I mean, at least I wasn't wearing wool shorts — calm enough to take in the big bulletin boards, glass doors, silvery water fountains.

"Take a look at all that chrome, Sal," Ruby nudged.

Girl →
looking
sick
in water
fountain

But when I looked at the chrome — which I knew I probably shouldn't — I mean, I was pretty sure that normal people did not look at chrome — all I could see was a slightly grey, slightly green girl with cotton shorts who looked, blurrily, right back at me.

Ouch.

Seemie:

I thought I feel happier in attic. Especially with half a bagel in my tumtum. But times gone by wash over me so bad — bagel also kind of heavy — that I slump down on Betty's box.

'A is for Apple. B for ...' I whimper to myself. I remember Sally, rrr-Miss Sally, teaching me so much. I remember her nose in Dictionary sniffing out 'bannister.' I look to sad desk where big red book still sit.

Wait a second.

I stand up, give myself good shake.

Just because I don't go to school don't mean I can't learn! I have books! And not just any book, I have rrr-Dictionary!

And with Dictionary, I can learn everything A for, and B, and C and all the way down to that last one, what is it? Rrr-Z!

I grin. I wag.

Then stop.

Because there one little problem.

.

XIII.

Sally:

Now, we walked into an old section of the building. This wasn't nearly so chrome-covered. Which was sort of a relief. (At least, my mom might stop nudging me.)

The bad part was that the kids here were all pretty much my own age, which meant....

"Here we are!" Ruby said.

In my terror, I tried to stick next to Pradip. (If there were two of us who didn't know anything, maybe at least half of the kids would stare at him.)

"That must be Ms. Burke," he whispered. Instead of pointing, he tilted the side of his hand towards a woman who stood in the center of some desks.

The woman made my blood run cold. Maybe it was her hair, a blonde helmet, or her heavily made-up eyes, or her pantsuit which was pink and gold, her earrings, which were pink and gold, her big pink and gold round pin, pink and gold purse, pink and gold — yes, even those — shoes.

I thought instantly of all the stray socks, gloves, mittens, my mom and I always wore because "they were still good."

Some of the socks my mom and I wore.

Shoes that matched her clothes that matched her earrings that matched her pin, and even, her lips, fingernails, eyes — I realized now that she had on pink eye shadow with gold eyeliner — seemed like a bad sign.

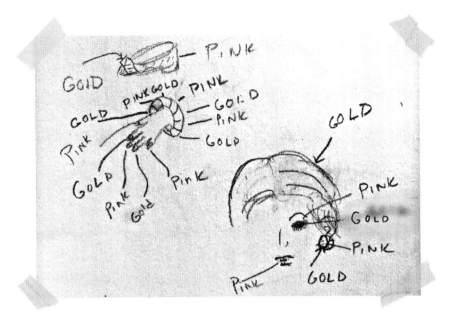

We could still go back to the truck, I thought, ready to drag my mom out.

Just then an older woman with light brown skin, short brown hair, pointy glasses, and a super straight back, said, "So, you must be Sally."

"Yyyes," I fumbled.

"And you must be Pradip," she continued, turning to him. "How nice you found each other already, since you're both new. I'm your teacher, Ms. Burke."

"*You're* Ms. Burke?" I sputtered.

Seemie:

The problem is how I get to Dictionary. The desk so high.

But there a chair at the back.

But it still a hard leap. Maybe I even get crushed....

I shut my eyes and think of Sally.

I shut my eyes and think "A", "B", "Z"....

Whoa! And here I am! Right on top of desk and, right next to me, sits the big red book! Webster's Coll ...

Coll ... Colle-gi-ate.

I step to side of Collegiate, and with flick of paw —
rrr-fifteen flicks of paw — raise cover.

Sally:

This Ms. Burke wasn't matching. I mean, all her stuff went together okay, but she didn't have the same color lipstick and earrings and shoe buckles and —

"I'm frightfully sorry," Pradip whispered to me. "But I'm also kind of relieved."

Me too, I thought, as I followed his gaze back to the lady in pink and gold. I could see now that she just happened to be standing in the middle of a group of desks, and that she did that because she was leaning over the shiny blonde girl from Scotto's.

I realized now that the blonde girl also matched her mom — at least, she was also dressed in pink and gold.

Their expressions also matched in a weird kind of way. Only at the same time, they also looked kind of the opposite of each other — what I mean is that the woman leaned over the girl, trying to talk her, while the girl leaned away from the woman, trying *not* to be talked to.

"Okay, Sal, sweets," my mom said.

'Mom!' I thought to myself. Only this 'Mom!' was not an irritated 'Mom,' or upset 'Mom,' or even a bored 'Mom.' It was an 'oh-no-don't-leave-me-Mom!'

I noticed then that Ruby's eyes were suspiciously sparkly. Like she too was a tearful little kid.

"Goodbye, Mom," I said, and before she could either (i) pull out a kleenex or (ii) wave, I turned back to the rows of desks.

Where I saw the blonde girl in pink and gold staring at me. I realized then that every time I'd seen that girl, her face had looked absolutely furious.

XIV.

Seemie:

ARGH!!!

If only I could start with A for Apple, I might be okay. But my paw took me to M for "MAL-A ... MALA ... COLOGY,"

And, sure, I guess M IS for MALA ... MALA ... COLOGY," but what is MALACOLOGY? Dictionary say it have to do with rrr-mollusks.

And M is also for "mollusks."

But what are rrr-"mollusks?"

I should be able to find out, I tell myself. I have

Dictionary right at my paws!

But there no way these paws can find "mollusks."

There no way these paws can find anything!

No wonder they don't let dogs in real school, I think

— dogs that can't even find mollusks!

So upset I let my head sink into the pages. The

pages so cold I am sure that my nose must be heating up. Meaning that I'm even getting sick from all this not-learning.

Then, just at the side of my hot nose, I see a dog.

Right there in the middle of that page! Right there in the middle of Dictionary!

"MALAMUTE," it say. "A sled dog of Northern North America, esp. ALASKAN MALAMUTE."

My head shoot up. I know about sled dogs — so brave, so strong, so rrr-sledfast — Sally and I read story once about them in home school.

And if sled dogs can charge through snow, then why can't me, Seemie, charge through pages! (My nose feel colder already.)

Then I notice that word "esp."

And my heart think — hey, Seemie, you act like you

are charging charging charging, but you don't even know

"esp" and it only have three letters.

Argh.

XV.

Sally:

School was weird. With a mom like mine, I was used to weird. The difference was that at school I was the weird one.

Actually, I'm not telling the whole truth here. School was not just weird, it was terrible. (But, yes, I *was* the weird one.)

It wasn't Ms. Burke's fault — she seemed to like me. Probably because that first day I was able to fix a smoke detector that kept going off and driving her crazy.

But some people — well, Raquelle, that blonde girl from Scotto's ice cream stand — hated me.

It seemed to start with a pencil. (Honestly, I don't think Raquelle liked me much even before the pencil, but afterwards....)

Raquelle liked chewing on pencils. This wasn't a big deal to me — my best friend is a dog.

But I guess Raquelle was embarrassed by her chewing. Because at one point, she threw one of her chewed pencils into the wastebasket — she had chewed it so hard that she bit it two. And I, thinking that she had dropped it by accident, fished it out of the waste basket and gave it back to her.

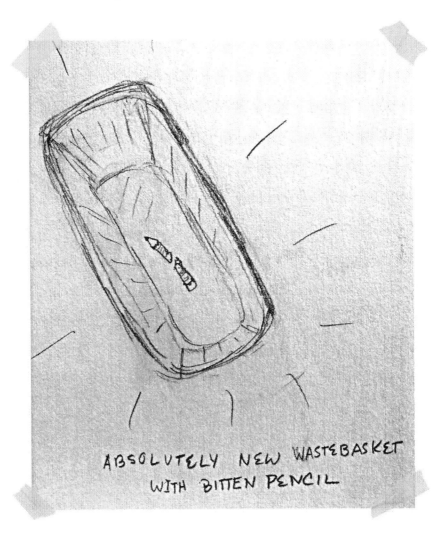

ABSOLUTELY NEW WASTEBASKET
WITH BITTEN PENCIL

Yes, I know. But, it was a perfectly new wastebasket, completely clean. (And, hey, I come from a house of recycling. I've helped Ruby sort materials from the dump. I get glasses of water under threat of donkey accordion and dented coffee pot.)

So, I picked up the pencil pieces and took them over to Raquelle, thinking I was doing her a favor.

NOT.

Seemie:

Sally so upset about her school that I don't tell her about dictionary.

"But you were just trying to help, Sal," I say, when she tell me about Raquelle.

"But she went ballistic."

"Balllisss?" (Argh!   Now, there's even a B word I don't know!)

"It means mad. Super mad. She threw the pencil pieces back in the wastebasket and actually yelled at me, 'keep your trash to yourself — ' Um...."

"She call a pencil, trash!!!?"

"Yes, but she also called me — well, a bad name."

"Like rrr-Leonard?"

"Not like Leonard," Sal whisper. "Like ... Garbage Girl."

Hmmm....

I like garbage. Sometimes, it have bits of sandwich. Even a cheese wrapper can still rrr-sport some real good goo.

But Sally different from me. I can tell that name makes her so sad.

Not a good time to ask what "ESP" is, I think. Instead, I snuggle into her side, making myself as warm as I can make me. (Except, you know, my nose.)

We stay like that for long while. Till finally I make myself ask — "rrr, Sal, can you think of way I turn pages?"

"Turn pages?"

"I think maybe I read a little when you're at school."

"Seemie, that's a great idea," Sally say. (Good Sal!) "Hey, I know. Mom made this automatic pageturner once. It's for people playing the piano, for music books. But I bet it would work on just regular books too."

Sal bring pageturner up to attic. I press the turning pedal with my paw and it turn just one page! (Not a pawful!)

Sally also bring a little stack of books for me to read. She set them up right next to the pageturner. Right next to Dictionary.

They look like comic books. I LOVE comic books.

But I am rrr-determined.   (Which, I soon learn, by

the way, begins with D.)

XVI.

Sally:

Before I started school, I thought I knew something about school — Seemie and I had played it enough. I soon realized that I didn't know anything.

"We should all be more careful about saving paper," Ms. Burke said, when I handed in all my work squeezed into the front, back and margins of a single page. (Like we always did at home.)

But it wasn't just school things I didn't know — I also didn't know kid things — TV programs, computer games, the latest toys, gadgets, music. Ruby and I only had a t.v. when she had one to fix. And though she let me use her computer, it really was *her* computer, the favorite websites all scrap metal places and scientific journals.

At least, I wasn't behind in most subjects. (Ms. Burke even called me a whiz in math.) There were two exceptions: spelling and Spanish.

In my home school, Ruby was always more interested in what I had to say than how I spelled it. Ms. Burke was different.

"If you can't spell correctly," she told our class, "people won't understand what you're trying to write. Even if they can understand you, they won't take you seriously. So, Class, proper spelling is simply something you are going to have to master this year."

Spanish was something Ruby and I had never studied at all. I told that to Señora Pangli, but she kept calling on me anyway.

Pretty soon I noticed that a lot of kids weren't much better than I was in Spanish. Pradip, who spoke at least three languages already (people in India just did, he said), spent the whole Spanish class looking for places to hide.

"You think Señora Pangli would notice if I slid under the desk?" he asked. (He sat next to me in class.)

"She might notice you're not here."

"Acha…. But what if I do it every day? So that she thinks

I'm *never* here? You could tell her I've dropped out. Or, wait, " his eyes widened. "You could tell her that I don't even exist. That that boy Pradip was a figment of her imagination."

Pradip was the one sort of bright spot of my day. The only problem was that Pradip was even weirder than I was.

Pradip was even wierder than me.

Okay, he got rid of the wool shorts after the first week of school and the navy blue tie by the end of the second week. Still, everyone imitated his accent. They made special fun of the Indian words he used like "acha," constantly saying "a-cha-cha-cha" and doing dumb dances behind him. A lot of kids called him "Dip," and the "Dipster," even though his name was actually pronounced Pra-deep (as in the *deep* blue sea.)

I never joined in on the teasing. But it still made me nervous. It felt like being teased was something you could catch, like a cold or some other bad germ.

The other problem with Pradip was that he was obsessed with Ruby's inventions. Back then, I carried around a few of her smaller gadgets — a self-cleaning eraser with the teeny dustbin and a battery-powered abacus. I had always liked these little inventions, but the way Pradip talked about them made me wish that I'd left them at home.

Then he got stuck on my backpack. "That is such an unusual napsack," he said. (Of course, he wouldn't call it a backpack!) "I bet your mom is right about the parachute silk — it has to hold up people's whole bodies. *And* in a strong wind. And to combine that with snakeskin —" He shook his head admiringly. "Ingenious."

Pradip had noticed the backpack before. What he did not notice — what he never seemed to notice — was Raquelle, Olivia and Gabby just behind him, listening to every word he said.

Later that afternoon, they pounced.

"Ooohh, Sally, that's such an unusual napsack," Gabby said, trying to imitate Pradip's voice..

"Yes," Olivia said, "there really is something ... very...."

"Acha," Raquelle sneered.

I was going to have to get myself another backpack, I told myself, just as soon as I could.

Unfortunately, that wasn't soon enough.

XVII.

Seemie:

Whew! A hard morning with old Noah. (Webster, that is.)

I rrr-encounter some really important words: BRIE. MUENSTER! Still, I fatigued. So take break in Ruby's workshop, eating crusts of her sandwich. (Good old Ruby.)

As I chew, Ruby rrr-inspect new machine. It look sort of like bicycle.

"The reversible seats even go side by side," she say, pushing them back-forth. "Pretty neat, huh, Seemie?

"The handlebars are centered." She touch bike's antlers.

"Baskets are on tight. You know who those baskets are for, don't you boy? I put a little piece of felt in each one too, so you'd be nice and comfy."

Me, comfy???

"Oh-oh," Ruby say, looking at clock. "We better hurry if we want to beat the bus."

But before I can hurry (and in opposite direction), Ruby pick me up and put me in front basket.

And before I can howl (better yet, jump down), she roll bike bumpity through workshop door.

"She's going to be really surprised, what do you think, boy?"

It tilt; it jerk; it sway! I try to cling to basket bottom, the bit of felt stuck there for my rrr-comfiness. But paws not made for clinging!

"It's okay, Seemie," Ruby rrr-croon. "Gee, I wonder if I should have made you some kind of seatbelt. But, you know what? If we crash, you'll probably be safer just jumping out."

If we crash!

She put one foot on pedal.

(She wouldn't!)

(She would!)

We move so fast I give up even pretending to cling. Just try to turn into curly bit of extra felt stuck to basket bottom. I'm too fat for felt, but what can I do? WHAT CAN I DOOOO???!!!

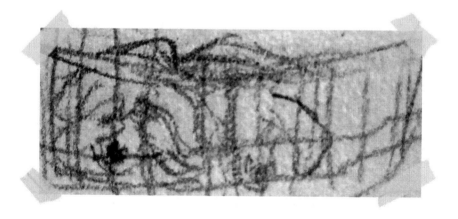

Wind whizz through fur, through stomach, through

heart. Wind whizz about a million mile per hour.

(Okay, Seemie. It can't really be a million mile per hour. A million is one thousand thousand. But even ten mile per hour is too fast for fat felt.)

Finally, we slow, we swerve — yeow! — we stop.

"Great. We haven't missed her," Ruby say.

Big spots in my mind clear to big bricks. Building. And, out of building, come kids! They aim toward yellow school buses.

Then, trudging out of double doors, her scent rrr-wafting toward me like late fall light.

I jump to hind legs, lean on basket, wriggle. Oh Sally Sally Sally good Sally!

"You see her, Seemie." Ruby say. "Ah, there she is. Sal!"

Sally heading for schoolbus, but now, she stop, she smile. I WRIGGLE!!!.

Then, all sudden, smile fade.

"What do you think?" Ruby ask, when Sally come close.

"Mom —"

"When you said how you hated the bus —"

"But Mom," Sally whisper, running fingers over red middle of big bike. "I can't really ride a bike. Don't you remember how I fell and cut my knee last year?"

I can tell Sally upset. I think of mouthing words, 'this not my idea,' but Sally not so good at dog lip reading.

"Oh Sal," Ruby say. "A bicycle built for two's not hard. It's fun right from the start."

"Fun for the kids that laugh at me when we crash."

"Look, Sweetheart, why don't we just wait till all the kids clear out. I wouldn't mind going in to say hi to Ms. Burke."

That's it! Why not say 'hi Ms. Burke. Can you give us car ride home?'

"No," Sally sigh. "Let's just get it over with. Come on, Seemie."

She pick me up and put me into back basket, put on extra bike helmet, hitch leg over seat, shift weight, and —

Oh no oh no oh no oh no! We tilt! We swerve! We really swerve! We — we — we —

Move!

Breezes blow through my muzzle. Leaves, trees, mailboxes slip by so fast their smells mix just like stew.

"Mom, we're doing it. Seemie, we're doing it," Sally cry.

"It's fun, right?" Ruby laugh.

"It's terrific!' Sally shout. "You like it, Seemie?" Sally whisper.

It hard to say yes when even your fur's scared stiff.

Honk! says school bus. (Yeowwwwww!!!!!)

All sudden, Sally start to sing.

"Daisy, Daisy," she sing.

Soon, Ruby join in. And now, "See-mie, See-mie," they sing. "Give me your answer true."

My answer? But what's the question?

"I'm half crazy," they sing.

Boy, I think, you certainly are.

XVIII.

Sally:

The bicycle built for two was one of Ruby's best machines ever. It didn't hee, haw, or take up half a football field.

All the kids liked it too. Pradip, of course, went absolutely bonkers.

Which was all kind of terrific until....

Seemie:

It fourth day we ride to get Sally, and that boy grrr-Pradip come over again while Sally put on helmet.

Pradip, grrr, tall, tan — eyes like grrr night sky.

Okay, so, he smell nice enough. But Sally MY girl.

Besides, he call me "Fuzzy."

"Hi Pradip, how are you doing today?" Ruby ask.

"I'm very well, thank you, Mrs. Darma." Pradip answer so perfect grrrr. "How are you?"

"I'm fine, thanks."

"Hey, Fuzzy."

I (grrrr) look down.

But Pradip look down too; then crouch down.

"Mrs. Darma," he say, "might I ask where you got that back wheel from? The middle wheel, I mean, the back to the front bike?"

"I got the parts from all over Fallsburg actually. Some from yard sales. Some, from people's garbage. Some, I even got from the dump. "

"From garbage?" Pradip say. "The poor do that in India, of course, and it's quite remarkable what they patch together, but I didn't realize people did it here."

"It's amazing what people throw out," Ruby say. "Real treasures."

"Um — Mom," Sally say and I sniff worry in her voice.

"Don't you think we should maybe...."

But before Sal can finish, Pradip start. "I was just wondering" he say, "because that metal piece over the chain looks just like part of my old bike. It said, '*Dynamite*,' just like that, in blue letters."

Ruby smile. "I always loved it when bikes said things like that."

"I know." Pradip smile too. (Grrrr.) "I loved that bike so much, we even brought it over from India. But then it got hit by the mail truck. They don't have big mail trucks like that in Delhi."

"So, maybe I used some of your bike," Ruby laugh.

"Gee, I'm really sorry. If I'd known it was yours, I could

have fixed it up like new."

Sally groan and all sudden unhappiness drape over her

like a rrr-drape.

I see then three girls. Just behind Sally. They have

hands over mouths, like hiding sharp teeth.

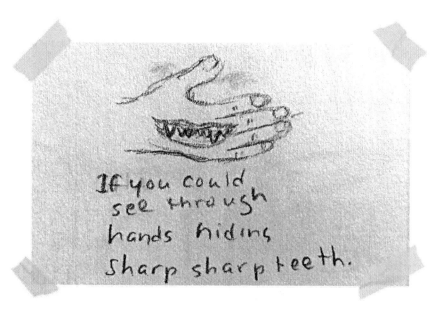

If you could
see through
hands hiding
sharp sharp teeth.

"Mom, can we just go?"

"That's what I'm here for," Ruby say. "Pradip, nice to

see you again. You should come out and visit some time."

"Mom, please."

Long, quiet ride home. No Daisy, no crazy, not a single answer true.

XIX.

Sally:

I prayed I was just being paranoid. Maybe they hadn't heard anything.

Even if they had heard — I mean, what was so bad about using bits of old bikes to make a new bike? It was good for the planet, right?

That's what I'd tell them. How good it was for the planet.

And, if they hadn't heard, then, well, I just wouldn't mention the planet.

But, of course, they had heard.

They'd also told the whole school. Raquelle, Gabby and Olivia were practically a walking website.

"Hey, Sal, you know that goofy bike your mom made, I'm

pretty sure it's got the back wheel from my old bike," Ritchie Parker shouted the minute I got on the bus. "Cause it said *'Stingray'* in rainbow letters. Just like yours. Boy, that was a crummy bike. It crashed me right into a stop sign, almost broke my arm."

As the morning went on, I also learned that one of the baskets on the tandem was from Lucy Jordan's big sister Natalie's bike. It was white plastic and said, *'Flyer'* on the side.

"They offered to give her old bike to me," Lucy said, "but it was so busted I didn't want it."

The front fender seemed to come from Sherelle Parson's mother's bike; "the one she got at a yard sale that didn't work."

It was Hazel Kandle's brother's bell. At least, she thought so. She couldn't be sure though, she said, so could she check it out when my mom brought it back to school. And if it *was* her brother's, she'd really like to get it back, she said: "after all, he's *my* brother."

Roman Delavega swore that my seat was from his babysitter's old exercise bike. "And that sure never seemed to work," he said, "cause my sitter was fat, man, fat."

Everyone thought that was especially funny — that I rode on a seat that had belonged to Roman's fat babysitter.

At recess, Raquelle, Gabby and Olivia surrounded me.

"Hey, Garbage Girl — we just figured out what was so *ingenius* about your backpack," Raquelle said. "You know all those weird colored patches all over the place? They look *exactly* like an old snakeskin purse of Olivia's grandmother's. Course hers was really old and mucked-up."

I looked down at my feet.

"God, I hated that purse," Olivia said. "It always smelled like mothballs and if my grandma gave you a mint or anything, it tasted of mothballs. You had to spit it out."

"Course your mother *made* that backpack, didn't she? So, it couldn't have anything to do with that stinky old purse Oliva's grandma threw out, could it, Garbage Girl?" Raquelle said.

If you ever want to know all about the lines circling the rubber rim of my right sneaker, and how one little place on front showed darker blue than the rest as if there was some extra glue on it, I can tell you exactly.

Though I realized, as I stared down at them, that even my

sneakers were weird. Ruby had sewed a funny little purple pocket onto one of them where I could stick some emergency money.

I quickly looked up again. Even though I couldn't stand looking at Raquelle, Gaby and Olivia, it was better than having them following my eyes to my sneakers. Inside, I screamed at my mom. Why did she have to make all these crazy junky things?

And Pradip! I screamed inside at him too. Why did he always have talk about all her crazy junky things?!

"Are you okay, Garbage?" Raquelle asked. "Your face is all red."

"It's sort of like your hair," Gabby said, shaking her perfectly straight, perfectly black, perfectly shiny, curtain bang. "Only redder."

"Gee, Garbage, you want me to get you some make-up?" Raquelle asked. "My mom probably has some stuck to the bottom of a bottle she's throwing away."

I rode the bicycle home one more time. Then told my mom I never wanted her to bring it to school again, and that I wasn't going to take the backpack anymore either, or any of the other weird junk she'd made.

I also told her that I wasn't going back to school myself.

"I've tried it now and I don't like it."

My mom was very sorry. She said she understood. She would even let me buy a brand new backpack, she said, whatever I needed.

But she would not let me quit school.

"School," she said, "is something that takes a little while to get used to."

I cried, I admit it. I cried, I begged, I pleaded.

She just kept saying that I'd have to give it more time.

XX.

Seemie:

A ruff night.

But, now, morning reach out its "rrr-rosy fingers of dawn" (that from Dictionary sentence sample), and I sniff blueberry pancakes. Ruby making something special for Sal.

And maybe for me too!

I wait for Sally. But instead of going downstairs, she keep going into Ruby's room and closing the door.

"Sal," I whimper, scratching door bottom. (I hate

closed doors.)

She open it just enough for me to come in, then close it again.

(I wish she not do that.)

Then I notice that she stare at back of door, a long glass there. Usually, a bathrobe hang over that glass.

"Sal, what you doing?"

"I just thought I'd try to get a head start on what they're going to laugh at today," Sally say.

"Huh?"

"Raquelle will find something no matter what, but I thought maybe — if I really check myself out before I leave—" She push her red fur behind ears.

"What you mean, 'check yourself out'?"

"Oh, Seemie, you know. Look at myself in the mirror."

"The mir-rrr-ror?"

Sally laugh, then stand me on two hind legs. "That's a mirror, see. And there," she tap a place on glass, "that's you."

Hey! The glass has pictures! One is a hand rrr-attached to … oh yeah, an arm. I follow arm to shoulder to head, which — oh wow! — look just like Sally's head.

"See there — one little mushki standing right up," Sally say, knocking again on glass.

Wait a second. That fuzzy … that curly … that white and grey and black….

"It don't smell like me."

"It's not the real you, Seemie. It's your — uh — reflection."

Honk!

"Oh Seemie, I wish I didn't have to go," Sally say.

But before she can even give me one last good pat, she hurry up downstairs.

Normally, I run after her. Normally, I stand at front door and WAVE WAVE WAVE her go. But this morning, I feel like deer in headlights, only it is me in mir-rrr-ror.

I know I have white curly fur. I can just look at paws to see that! But my face — it's furry too. And so puffy!

Sally and Ruby always say I'm cute, but I look like a little rrr-airhead!

When I pant, my tongue stick out. A lot.

I pull tongue in, shut mouth tight.

I don't even want to think about the sight of me rolling over to get my tumtum rubbed.

I think of Pradip. So clothed, so rrr-dignified.

Grrrr....

XXI.

Sally:

I wasn't talking to Pradip ever again, but he didn't seem to notice, following me constantly and jabbering away.

At recess, I tried hiding behind a comic book. Pradip sat down right next to me.

"Hi Sally. You want to play that game, Boodies?" (That was a game we made up that Pradip said was sort of like cricket, which was a game he played in India.) "You're getting really good at it."

I stared hard into my comic book.

"Aa — cha," Pradip said.

At last, he was quiet.

But only for a minute.

"Sally," he said. "I'm terribly sorry about that Dynamite business. I should have known better, kept my lips sealed. I guess I just couldn't help myself. The things your Mum makes are so terrific."

I had meant never to look at him again, but here I simply had to shoot him a glare.

"Sally, everyone gets teased sometimes," he went on. "Everyone that's at all interesting. Look at me. Well, I may not be so interesting, but…."

"Pradip, please. Can't you just leave me alone?"

He sighed, then looked back over his shoulder. "Listen, this is a secret. I'll tell you if you want."

I did not want.

"I think I got so excited about all your mom's inventions because I'd like to be an inventor myself someday. Only, in my family, everyone's, you know, a pharmacist.

"I certainly didn't mean to cause you a problem." He shook his head slowly. "You're the one person I've met I really like."

Why couldn't he ever shut up!? Pretty soon they'd be

singing, "Garbage Girl and Dipster Sitting in a Tree." And it would be his fault all over again.

I got up and walked as fast as I could to the other side of the playground, right by the school building, then slumped down onto the sidewalk, sticking my face back into my comic book.

About a minute later, I heard a slump right next to me.

"Pradip, don't you get it? Leave me alone!" I said, as I looked up to a warm dark face with pointy eyeglasses.

Seemie:

I try to get away. Upstairs to sit by the Dictionary or downstairs to stand by the Fridge. By Fridge and blueberry pancake bits.

But the mirror is like a chocolate steak, holding me even as it make me sick.

Finally, I pull myself away and run upstairs. I leap on pageturner, desperate for new good words.

But the pageturner don't just click.

I press pedal again.

And again.

Still, nothing happen!

"Pageturner!" I growl and pounce on pedal even harder.

But pedal pull away from pages and clunk down onto floor. It thud. It shake.

"Please, Pageturner," I whimper.

"Please," I bark, growl, WAVE WAVE WAVE.

But pageturner won't listen.

Finally, I bend down over the Dictionary and try turning pages myself. Claws don't work so I bite bite bite under pages — when, all sudden — yeow! — the Dictionary bites back! Bites my little black nose!

I try to lick it.

But my tongue won't reach my nose, and also ... I rrr-imagine how dumb my tongue look.

So, I stop. Even though my nose in rrr-agony. But what can I do? WHAT CAN I DOOOO???

I wonder — I can't help myself — what would Pradip do?

Oh, Pradip probably just bandage stupid nose. But stupid paws don't just bandage.

I limp downstairs. Climb onto couch. Sniff Sally's shampoo on top cushion, lean paws so careful against her sweater left there.

Look out window. Watch branches of old willow tree rrr-tease tire stacks. Press my poor hurt nose against the glass.

After a while, my nose hardly sting any more. But the rest of me still feel deeply rrr-wounded.

XXII.

Sally:

"What a day," Ms. Burke said, squinting above her smile.

"Gee, uh," I said, stumbling to my feet. "Would you like me to get you, um, a chair?"

"No thanks," Ms. Burke said, patting the sidewalk next to her. "It's kind of nice to sit on something solid for a change. Some of those school chairs are so tippy, they're like a rocker with legs."

Was that supposed to be a joke? Since I wasn't sure, I tried to laugh, but not too hard.

"You like comics?" she asked, with a nod towards my book.

"Sort of," I said. "But I'll put it away," I added. "If they're not allowed."

"Nah, that's okay. I used to love comics," she said.

"You can borrow it if you want."

"No, thanks," Ms. Burke said again, then reached over to look at the cover, "Well, maybe, I will sneak a peek later. But that's not why I came over here to talk to you."

Oh-oh. She'd come over to talk for a reason.

"It's hard being a new kid," Ms. Burke said. "Actually, it's hard being a new anything. A new pair of shoes is about the worst."

I guessed that was another joke, but somehow I couldn't get another 'ha' out.

"I, for one, used to get blisters every single September. I liked those big wedgy things." Her nose crinkled in distaste.

"Oh," I tried.

"But what I was thinking, Sally.... Well, I heard you've had some problems about a certain bicycle."

I groaned.

"But it sounds so wonderful," Ms. Burke smiled. "The fact your mom built it! Now, my mother, she could sew, but she could never really do anything mechanical. My dad — he could change a tire, but that was about it. To be able to work with machines is a great gift."

I groaned again.

"That bike makes me think of a story of something that happened to me when I was a kid. Do you mind if I tell it to you?"

I did kind of mind. All I wanted was the world to leave me alone. But I knew she was trying to be nice, so, "okay," I said.

Ms. Burke looked out over at the playground, but I could tell she wasn't really seeing it. She was looking out the way my mom did when she was trying to picture a new machine, only in her case, she seemed to be trying to picture a memory. She even adjusted her pointy glasses, as if to see it better.

Then, she told me a long story about a coat she had when she was a girl in school, and how, for some reason, the other kids had teased her about it, even after her mom, who was such a good sewer, tried to specially decorate it. The kids had bothered her so much, she had finally just gotten a new coat, even though her family didn't really have a lot of money for extra coats, and how that had made them put off getting other things they always wanted, like, it turned out, a piano.

It was a sweet story, and I knew Ms. Burke was telling it to make me feel better. But all I could think about was that she just had a problem with a coat, or maybe with a piano, or a coat *and* a piano, while I had a problem with my whole life.

coat ≠ whole life

XXIII.

Seemie:

I jump down at last and limp to Ruby's room, back to that awful mir-rrr-ror. (It only my nose that is hurt; still, I feel need to limp.)

I look myself in the eye, rrr-mir-ror's eye.

From now on, I vow to be different.

I can't change fur. Or puff. But no sniffing, rolling, hanging out of tongue.

I will be a friend Sally is proud of. Someone she look up to. Rrr-down to. But, PROUDLY down to.

Even if it mean I no longer a Mushki!

(I bet she don't call Pradip silly names.)

(Grrr....)

Sally:

I was feeling pretty good about Ms. Burke after recess, even though her story about her coat didn't seem to have much to do with me.

Feeling pretty good, that is, until later that afternoon when she made an important announcement.

"Class," she said. "I'm happy to tell you that we're going to have our first spelling bee next Friday, and I think it's going to be great fun."

Ms. Burke! I thought, feeling completely betrayed.

"I can't imagine who's going to pick you on their team, Garbage Girl," Raquelle said from behind. "Unless one of the words is D-U-M-P."

It was like Raquelle had flicked a switch; like I was some machine Raquelle had turned on, a machine that instantly spat sparks.

"I may not be so great at spelling, Raquelle," I said. "And I may not have such great stuff. But you know what I have that *is* pretty great? I have this great dog — a dog who can talk, a dog who can actually *talk*."

I don't know what I expected. What happened was that Raquelle started laughing. Uncontrollably.

"Now, Garbage thinks she's taught her dog to talk!" she said, pulling on Oliva's braid as she doubled over. "Talk about an idiot."

Seemie:

Sally coming up walkway, but I will not pant.

Oooohhh — here she is here she is here she is!!!!!!!

Everything in me want to wriggle; everything in me want to hang out its tongue; everything in me want to give up on dognity — rrr — dignity — and roll over to show its tumtum!

"Bad dog!" I tell myself.

"Sit!" I rrr-insist!

Sally:

"What's wrong, Sal?" Ruby asked the minute I came home.

But Seemie just stared up at me. So still. So serious. It was like he already knew what I'd done.

"We're going to have a spelling bee." I blurted out. (I couldn't tell my mom the rest of it.) "And I can't spell anything right."

"Oh, Sal, you spell fine. You've just got to identify with the *positive*," Ruby sighed. "You know, that part of you that can spell."

"There is no part of me that can spell."

"The problem not you, Sal," Seemie whispered as we climbed to the attic. "It the English language. It so rich, see. It got words from just about every other tongue in the world. That's what old Noah say."

"Noah?"

Seemie — seriously — blushed, the skin under his curls turning so pink that he looked like a walking peach.

"Noah rrr-Webster. He wrote dictionary," Seemie said. "And I've been reading it."

"You've been reading the Dictionary?"

I looked down at the little mushki. There he was, hopping on all fours up the attic stairs, just like a regular dog — a regular dog who was part peach.

"Seemie, that's incredible. Reading the dictionary?! How do you even do it?"

"Rrr-well, I hook it up to Pageturner, and — I sorry, Sal — it fell."

We stepped into the attic and I noticed for the first time that the dictionary open, but at a weird tilt, and down on the floor below it, sprawled the pageturner.

"Wow! Seemie! You used the pageturner?" I bent down and righted it again. I fitted it back into the dictionary. "And, so now, you're a really good speller?"

Seemie's tail began to wag. Only not.

I mean, it seemed to wag and stop and wag and stop and half-wag and stop. (I couldn't help noticing how strange that was even though I wasn't actually focusing on Seemie's tail. I mean, my dog had been reading the dictionary! That was strange enough!)

"I *rrr-moderately* good speller," Seemie said.

"Can you spell something for me right now? I don't know, like...."

"How about 'rrr-antidisestablishmentarianism'?"

"Anti-what?"

"'Rrr-disestablishmentarianism.'"

"How about it?"

Seemie sat up straight. I mean, he sat down straight — I mean, you know, he sat the way dogs do. Then, after a deep breath, "rrr-A-N-T-I-D-I-S-rrr-E-S-T-A-B-L-I-S-rrr-H-M-E-N-T-A-rrr-R-I-A-N-I-S-M!" he spelled.

I admit it. This was weird.

"Seemore," I said. "How did you learn all that?"

"When you were my teacher, Sal. You know, A is for apple. That's why I sure you can learn too."

It seemed impossible — a dog reading the dictionary. *My* dog reading the dictionary.

Trying to understand it, I sat on the floor and just patted Seemie for a while. "You are one funny little Mushki," I said. "But, the best," I added quickly, because Seemie still seemed so stiff and weird and serious, not even stretching into my pat.

Of course, reading something like the dictionary might make you sort of serious, I thought, eyeing the huge book. Then my eye landed on something else sitting on the desk. Two things actually — they were small, shiny, metallic.

"You just need practice, Sal," Seemie said. "Then you do great in spelling bee."

"Sure," I said slowly. But what I thought about just then was not exactly spelling practice.

Seemie:

When Sally tell me how I can help her, I get so confused I nearly start to pant again.

I try to calm down. When in doubt, I tell myself, go back to old Noah. I scan through all the C words filed inside my brain.

'Cheating,' I remember: '1. to deprive of something rrr-valuable by use of deceit or rrr-fraud; 2. to influence or lead by deceit, trick or arti...arti...arti-something; 3. to violate rules dishonestly (as in a contest or an examination).'

Oh no! 'Cause a spelling bee's kind of contest, right? Or, an examination?

Which mean that what Sally is asking me to do isn't

just any old cheating. It part of the definition of

cheating!

I feel both ARGH and YEOW at once.

Then I feel something wet drop on my head. (Not

the Plantwaterer!)

"Seemie, you don't have to help me," Sally say, wiping her eyes. "It doesn't matter if the kids know I'm stupid — they already think I'm an idiot."

"You not stupid, Sal."

"But I just can't spell in front of people," she sigh.

"Rrr-listen Sal," I say, " I help you." (For she is my good Sal, no matter what Noah say.) "But you got to study really hard anyway. You got to pretend that I rrr-refuse to help."

"Oh, you little mushki — you are the best dog ever," Sally say, giving me big hug.

Sal so happy, a part of me want to roll over and get my tumtum rubbed right now! But another part, the part that still see that C word in its head, just wants to run and hide!

XXIV.

Sally:

I usually woke up these days dreading school. The next day, I woke up dreading myself.

I had come up with a pretty complete plan by then, a plan using Seemie, my one-way walkie-talkie, a collar, and some earrings I was going to rig up — yes, earrings — I couldn't think of anything else — and the big parachute silk backpack.

It was a plan that made me hate myself.

Because it was wrong. Even if it could work. Which it probably wouldn't. I mean, seriously — earrings!

Still, I was so busy thinking about it all that I forgot I had told Raquelle that Seemie could talk. Until I got on the bus and Stephanie

Kandle shouted out at me, "hey, Sally, can you teach *my* dog to talk?"

Ritchie Parker barked "arf arf," holding up his hands like paws.

When we got to school, Raquelle and her crew greeted me with calls of "Garbage Doolittle." Which, of course, everyone else immediately picked up.

Everyone, that is, except Pradip and Ms. Burke. But I avoided them — Pradip, because I was never talking to him again, and Ms. Burke, because I was planning to cheat in the spelling bee.

Because that morning decided me for sure. I mean, I'd study, just like Seemie wanted. But I was going to make the best walkie-talkie earrings anyone had ever made.

Seemie:

I hoped it not come. I hoped there would be flood, earthquake, fire. I hoped that maybe Sally would break leg, or I would break leg or Ms. Burke break leg.

But here it is: Friday morning — day of spelling bee — and everybody's legs okay.

Sally give me great early breakfast — english muffin with butter and raspberry jam.

But I so nervous I can hardly eat.

Then Sally let me outside. Morning is clear, grass stiff with rrr-frost. Up in sky, a piece of moon still shows even in rosy-fingers-of-dawn light.

Normally, the sight of moon make me happy. When I was a pup, Sally and I read that the moon was made of cheese.

But the moon this morning does not look like any

cheese I know. Which makes me wonder if there are lots

of cheeses I don't know. And maybe lots of other things I

also don't know. Like the punishments they give to cheater

dogs.

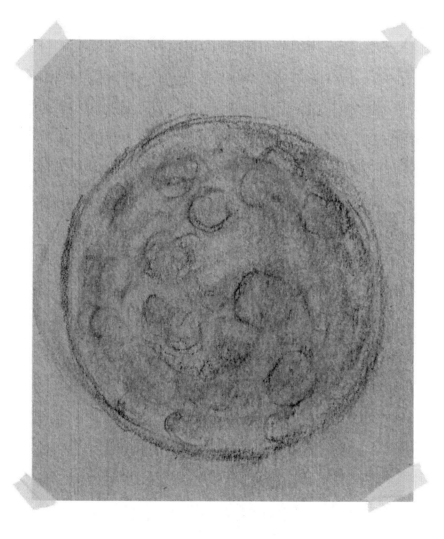

"Seemie," Sally call, and her voice shiver as much as me. And though I want to run away, I know I have to come, for Sally is my girl.

"We better do it out here," she say, bending down with walkie-talkie piece for collar. "And I think we better keep both sides of the walkie-talkie off until just before the Spelling Bee. okay? Then I'll just reach into the pack and click it on."

I try to nod but she pulling collar right into my nodding place. (Argh.)

Then she unzip backpack and lay it on the ground. It look like just like a lump of lumpy cloth down there.

I make myself squeeze into lumpy inside space. It dark and smell of ... hmmmm....

"You're set?" Sally whisper.

"Rrr — yes," I whisper back. (I so good at that now — all this week while Sally practice spelling, I practice dog whispering.)

I think I all set, but when Sally pick up pack — YEOW! I slide — ARGH — onto neck, bite tongue.

"Seemie, are you okay?" Sally cry, her face in backpack even bigger than morning moon.

I taste blood, which I don't mind in steak, but don't much like in backpack. But Sally's face so big look so upset.

"I rrr-fine," I say.

XXV.

Sally:

Sally, I kept telling myself, you don't have to do this. Then —
so fast — the bus honked, my mom gave me a quick kiss, and
Seemie and I were on our way.

I took a seat by myself. (That part was easy since no one
wanted to sit with Garbage Doolittle.)

After checking to make sure no one was watching, I took the
walkie-talkie earrings from one of backpack pockets, and stuck them
on my ears.

They pinched. A lot. But — I shook my head — at least, they
shouldn't fall off.

Transistor earring.

Seemie:

The motor goes brmm. The kids go BRRRM. I try to

focus on the backpack but there not much to see.

(Backpacks don't come with a view.)

Snakey at bottom, silky in middle — sides and top all rough — also snakey.

Ooh, nose itch.

I try to scratch it against pack side, when all sudden bus sway and I got bigger problem than itchy nose. Sally's english muffin bounce in my tumtum, bounce up way too high —

I need air I need air I need air.

I get up, circle.

"Seemie, stop it!" Sally whisper, zipper-mouthed.

"But I sick."

"Seemie, you never get car sick."

"But we not in car."

"Oh, right, oh gee — Can't you just last a few more minutes?"

As I try to say yes, I hiccup. It must be a big hiccup

for a little dog because Sally unzip pack fast, reach down,

pat me. (Good Sally.)

"I know it was in here somewhere," she say all loud.

"Oh, Seemie, I hope this helps," she whisper, putting the opening of pack next to bus window.

The window so cool, the English muffin feel better right away.

Bus is almost nice like this, almost sleepy, almost....

WHAM — YEOW! Turn turn tur — rrr — n shake (argh!) stop.

"Hey!" someone shout.

"Come on," someone yell.

"No wonder you get bad grades if you do your homework on the bus," someone say.

Below all talk, I hear that BRRRM BRRMM BRRRM again. Now, it sound like a great big drum — the drum they beat when prisoners march the plank. Which I realize, as Sally zip up, is not the BRRMM of kid anymore, not even the bus BRRMM — it the drum of my own heart.

It so loud loud loud, the whole world must hear it!.

Oh no!

Oh no!

Oh no!

XXVI.

Sally:

So, we're here now. Seemie and me. Me and Seemie. And only about a zillion kids.

Seemie:

Elephants. Rhinos. Rrrr-wildebeests!

Brrmm brrmm CRASH!

Brrmm brrmm BANG!

Wait a second! But there also ketchup! Sniff, floor soap, sniff, paper, pencils, MORE ketchup, sniff and lots

— LOTS — of shampoo.

And heat, sniff. From rrr-radiators.

So much heat, it have its own smell.

(So different from home. Ruby, loving planet, keep heat low.)

Thump, ouch. Bang, ouch. YEOW (silently).

But — brrmm brrmm brrmm — there are just too many feet in this hot heat — yeow yeow (silently.)

Sally:

I had gotten used to how busy school was, but with Seemie on my back, the kids all seemed to be bumper cars, bumper cars determined to crash into us. I pulled the pack to the front of my body, holding one arm over it as a shield, then steered us towards a deserted hall, right next to a dusty bulletin board where they put up all the PTA news.

It was quiet there, empty. I unzipped the top of the pack. "You okay, Seemie?" I whispered down.

"I rrr — okay, Sal."

I tried to relax. Seemie was okay; Seemie would be okay, I told myself.

Just as I was almost believing that, a voice bright as a kitchen light at midnight, said, "Sally Darma! Good morning!"

It was Pradip, of course, the one person who was sure to notice, loudly, that I was carrying my old backpack. Knowing Pradip, he'd probably even spot the walkie-talkie in my right earring.

I flipped my hair over my ear as I turned my face farther away from Pradip. (I was not only not talking to Pradip; I was also not looking at him.)

Pradip sighed. "Today's the day for that spelling bee, right? Did you study?"

I turned my head further away, trying to infuse the message 'go away,' into my hair.

"You'll probably stay in until the end anyway," Pradip said. "I just keep telling myself that at least it's not in Spanish."

I made myself stare at the PTA news.

"By the way," Pradip went on. "I don't think my laryngitis

trick has been working very well with Señora Pangli. And *you* haven't helped much with pretending I don't exist...."

Pradip went silent.

Me too.

Well, *I'd* already been silent, but this new silence was different. This new silence wasn't even very quiet; instead, it was a silence that seemed to shout at me. What it shouted was that I was being mean.

I took a deep breath. I made myself turn my head around, this time towards Pradip. I made myself — well, *let* myself — look at him.

He looked so sad. His forehead shadowed, shoulders hunched — even his long nose seemed droopy.

"You know, I'm really sorry about that," I said, throwing in a half-smile (you know, the embarrassed kind.)

Which made Pradip smile too. Only his was a whole smile. The toothy kind (but also kind of sweet.)

"*Acha*," he laughed.

Seemie:

Sally stop, talk, and now she walk again, swing us through air again. And now — ouch — she plop us down on something hard, rrr-slide us....

It darker here. Sally bend down, unzip pack. Just a little, but enough that I can see: silver sides of zipper, other metal, some pale wood, blue. Not sky blue — Sally's blue jean blue.

It warm down here, even a little rrr-snug.

Sally's hand slip down to pat me.

"Mmmm," I sigh.

"Ssshhh," she whisper.

XXVII.

Sally:

I had somehow expected that the spelling bee would be the first thing in the morning. After that, I'd pretend I didn't feel well (I wouldn't have to pretend very hard the way my ears hurt) and Seemie and I would go home early.

But when I looked at the schedule on the board, I saw that the words "Spelling" and "Bee" (with little daisies on either side) were at the very bottom. The only thing later was "Clean Up to Go Home."

"Earrings, Doolittle?" Raquelle said, sidling up to me. "Are they giving them away free at the dump? Tell me, do they give them to just anybody, or only people who can talk to animals?"

I didn't answer, though I could feel my ears grow red. (Make that, redder.)

I could also feel that secret wish rise inside me again. If only I could just show her that I really did have a talking animal. That would teach her. That would teach all of them.

Seemie:

It a little hard to hear so snug under desk; me kind of sleepy too, after bus trip. But every once in while I catch bits of Ms. Burke's voice: "Math books," "page 57," "quiet now, kids."

Her voice remind me of some other voice.

"Can't we just use our calculators?" someone shout.

"No, you cannot use your calculators," Ms. Burke say — standing, it seem, by Sally's desk. (She smell of rrr-lavender —)

Then it get so quiet, so still, so ... for a long

tiiimmmme............

RRRINNNNG.

A wind! It bang, rrr-ruffle, scrreeech —

"I'll be just a minute Ms. Burke," Sally say, and then

... and then ... all sudden ... wind hush and Sally's face peer

in, her big backpack face.

"You're doing a great job, Seemie. Oh my gosh, you

little mushki. Are you okay in there?"

"It a bit rrr — cramped and aaa-aaa-tccch —" I

need to sneeze.

"Aaaa-aaaa-ttchh —"

"You are just amazing," Sally say, and push her whole

face in, giving me kiss.

It is really cramped with her whole face in there.

But I don't mind.

Sally:

"Hey, Doolittle, Ms. Burke says to hurry up," says Gabby, coming back to the door.

And there I am talking to Seemie, my head in the backpack.

"I'm coming," I shout, and raise my head so fast I nearly

wham my head into the desk.

Which somehow makes me feel even worse inside.

Seemie:

Sniff! This must be lunchroom. Where all the ketchup come from. Yum!

Even though Sally make no promise about food, I feel all sudden so happy. Partly it's the ketchup, sure, but also it's the change of scene.

Okay, so I am still in backpack! But at least in this scene I hear chewing.

Talking too. So much talking I can hardly pick out separate words — but — aaaahhh — here some:

"Look! Now, she's bringing that stupid backpack to lunch," some girl say.

I can smell even through ketchup that that girl is not a nice girl.

"Maybe she's afraid someone will steal it," laugh another not-nice girl.

"MAYBE she's afraid they'll throw it out." (That one — sniff — is Raquelle! — the most not-nice girl.)

I need to growl. It only the sniff of all that ketchup

that stop me — good ketchup, good ketchup — aaaa —

aaaa — aaaa —

Ttchoo!!!

All sudden Sally on the move again. Sally, no!!!

Goodbye, Ketchup!

XXVIII.

Sally:

It felt too dangerous to stay in the lunchroom with Seemie on my back, but the only other place I could think to go was the girls' restroom.

The trouble with the girls' restroom was that the whole first grade was in there, and when they were done (after forever), my lunch period was almost over.

I took the pack into one of the toilet stalls, and pulled Seemie out through the top, hoping to at least let him get some air, even bathroom air. Instead, when I got the little mushki on my lap — which, okay, was awkward — all he could do was shake and sneeze.

"Seemie, are you all right?"

"I must be rrr-allergic, Sal, to ah-ah-ah — tchoo —"

"Not the silk, Seemie."

"Not the silk, the aaaahh — snake — tchoo!"

"The snakeskin?"

"But it okay. Rrr-at least, out here." Seemie looked around. "Sally, where *is* out here?"

"It's the girls' restroom."

"But, Sally! I a boy!"

"Seemie! You're a dog! Nobody is going to see you in here anyway."

"You're not going to let me get down? Not one paw to rrr-earth!"

"It's tile, Seemie, bathroom tile. And if anyone comes in here, they'll tell —"

"Rrr-oh-oh-oh-tchoo!"

I patted Seemie, trying to calm his shakes and sneezes. But all I could think of was someone seeing us, then running to tell. Only, instead of it being bad, it was kind of wonderful — everyone, you know, thinking we were so cool.

"Seemie, listen, I know you're worried about dog scientists."

"They always say it not going to hurt," Seemie shivered.

"I know," I went on patting him. "But, um, how would you feel — you know, if someone *did* tell?"

"Tell?"

"That you can talk."

"Rrrr...."

"And what if that someone —"

"Rrr..." Seemie whispered.

"What if that someone," I whispered back. "Was ... me?"

Just then, the door whisked open.

"Hey, Garbage," sneered Raquelle. "Ms. Burke wonders what you're doing in here."

"Oh geeze. I'm ... just ... uh...."

"She says, unless you're sick, which we know you are," Raquelle laughed, "to hurry it up already. And leave the trash cans alone!"

The door whisked shut again, Raquelle's mean laugh magnified by its swing, then echoing, with her footsteps, down the hall.

Seemie and I waited a full minute before talking, maybe even before breathing. (At least I couldn't hear any breathing. Only the drip of a leaking faucet.)

Then, silently, quickly, I helped Seemie back into the pack. Just as I started to zip, he stuck his little head out .

"Sal, rrr-about rrr-telling," he stammered softly. "You ... rrr ... should ... you rrr-should do what you think is rrr-right ."

"Seemie, we've got to hurry," I said.

Seemie:

I try not to think about it. I try just to be happy that it more airy out in playground. Wait a second! What that?

Oh. Sally's hand, and piece, yum, of peanut butter sandwich.

Good Sal.

I love peanut butter, but it thstick to my muthzzle and make me lick my lips and, wait — Sally's fingers. Dripping with water. Good girl, good girl, Sally!

All sudden I hear that voice again.

"I guess your mom hasn't gotten around to inventing the napkin," Raquelle say.

A growl push my throat. I push it (with my muzzle) down into pack bottom.

Can't hear Raquelle down here. That good. But my nose also pushed into snakeskin. Aaahhhhh — aaaahhh

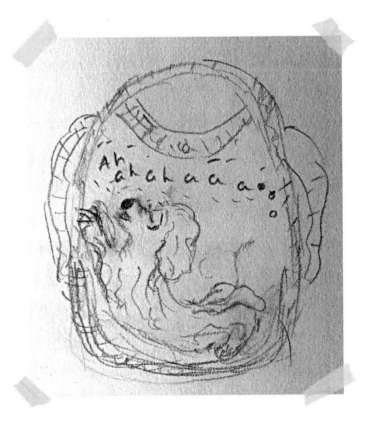

Aaaaa — aaaa —

TCHOO!!

YEOW!!!

Sally swing us UP UP UP and AROUND, and then after she walk walk walk — DOWN.

"Seemie," Sally whisper, her lips make zipper crack pink. "I really am trying to keep people from finding out about you. But if you make noise —"

"I aaa — aaa — aaaa — sorry, Sal," I say.

Sally is quiet a minute, reaching hand into pack, trying to pat (I think) my head, but getting my nose.

"Aaaaa — aaaa—" I answer.

"Wait a sec," she say. "What if I take off my sweater and stuff it over the snakeskin? You're not allergic to sweater, right?"

Then I feel Sally swish above us — me and pack. Then she open pack — we seem to sit down by her knees — and stuff sweater all around me, below me too.

"How's that?" she whisper.

It crowded. But before I can complain, another voice speak up. "Look at Garbage. Now, she's talking to her backpack."

"Yo, Garbage. What's in that pack anyway?" (That one is Raquelle.)

I feel Sally panic. I feel me panic, I feel a whole

bunch of fingernail polish closing in —

Then someone say, "Don't touch it, Raquelle! You'll smell all like mothballs."

"Yeah, Rachie, you'll smell just like her!"

"Eeeuwww," they all say.

But someone else don't say anything. That someone just GRRRR GRRRRR GRRRR GRRRR GRRRRRR!!! SO LOUD!

XXIX.

Sally:

I stuck my hand in the pack, found Seemie's muzzle, pressed my fingers around it, and said (with a calmness that amazed even me) , "I thought I'd turned that thing off."

Then I walked away. Fast. Keeping my hold on Seemie till I got (again) to the other side of the playground.

"Seemie," I said, trying to keep my lips straight so it wouldn't look like I was talking. "What are you doing?! You can't growl!"

"But, Sally, they were attacking you."

"Oh, Seemie. That's just how Raquelle and her gang are. You can't let it bother you."

"But rrr — you do, Sal," Seemie whispered. "You let it

bother you all time."

"Okay —" I started.

But what could I say?

"Oh, Seemie," I whispered, lips still stiff and straight.

"Good Sal," Seemie whispered back.

Seemie:

"Children, please settle down," come Ms. Burke's voice over rrr-din of chair chatter. "You don't have to talk to put up your jackets, do you? You need to get ready for Spanish!"

All sudden I know where I hear Ms. Burke's voice before! She sound just like Miss Sally!

Good Miss Sally!

Even though I still squeezed between silk and sweater, I feel the walls of old attic school open. Good old attic school!

Sally:

"Buenas Tardes, niños," Señora Pangli said. Then, she scanned the room for someone to call on. I looked down at my desk quickly, hoping she wouldn't catch my eye.

I even looked below my desk, hoping she wouldn't catch my forehead.   There, I caught the backpack.

It quivered slightly. Which, even though it made me nervous — *more* nervous — also somehow made me happy. Because it reminded me of the box at the pet store. Seemie's box.

Señora Pangli said, "Como se llama?

Okay, so I'd heard that one before. It meant something like … uh, what are you … how are you…?

No, *who* are you? That was it. *What's your name?*

Garbage Girl, I thought sadly, the one and only Garbage Girl, the one and only Cheating Garbage Girl.

Seemie:

Wow! All I know is English, Dog, and a little rrr-Aquarium.

But, Seemie, I tell myself, so stern. You can't study Spanish right now. What you have to do right now is think.

But all I can think is that those girls don't make fun of Sally spell, they make fun of how she smell!

Which is ridiculous! Because Sally smell great.

But that means — I thinking hard now — those girls won't like Sally even if she spell perfectly.

And if I spell for Sally, she won't spell at all. And that not good for Sally! Because spelling is good! And cheating — "to violate rules dishonestly — as in a contest or examination" — is not good!

And it my job as Sally's dog to save her from not-good stuff! You know, like — rrr ... like ... rrr....

Sally:

As I looked down at the quivering backpack, I remembered

how I had picked Seemie up out of the quivering cardboard box, and how, afterwards, on the way home, my mom and I had figured out a name for him.

Seemore. Seemie. Mushki.

But none of those things were who he really *was.*

"Como se llama?" Señora Pangli said, right next to me. I looked up and saw that she was pointing to Pradip, who looked blank and blinked. (He was trying, I guessed, to blink his way to an answer.)

I don't know what got into me, but I raised my hand — not I hoped in a show-offy way.

"Sally," Señora Pangli smiled. "Como se llama?" She pointed to Pradip.

Huh?

Oh yeah, she was asking me what *his* name was.

"Pradip," I said. "He, I mean — *el* — se llama Pradip."

"Bien, muy bien," Señora Pangli said. "Y como se llama usted?" This time, pointing towards me.

"What? Oh. Uh … Sally Darma. *Yo* … me llamo Sally Darma."

Pradip smiled at me then, raising one hand to his head, which he pretended to wipe with relief.

"Muy bien, Sally," Señora Pangli said, smiling too. "Tu hables español muy bien."

Now, she was telling me that I spoke Spanish ... very well.

"Gracias," I said. (Pradip threw me another whew! face, trying, I realized, to thank me.)

And then I realized something else.

I was not Garbage Girl. That was just a name.

Okay, Sally Darma was also just a name. But it was *my* name.

And even though I didn't know exactly who Sally Darma was, I knew who she wasn't — she was not someone who cheated. She was also not someone who would betray her dog, against his wishes, even if it would make people think she was cool. That just wasn't who she — *I* — was.

Then a wave of my own whew! washed over. Because now I knew what I was going to do. At least, I knew what I *wasn't* going to do.

Seemie:

All sudden I feel like an esp. Alaskan Malamute, refusing to carry his girl over thin ice, across broken bridge, into a burning igloo—

Burning igloo

Burning igloo!?

Oh, Seemie.

Any minute Sal will reach for your collar; any minute she will turn on walkie-talkie — your girl, Sal! Any minute you are supposed to listen up good and whisper whisper —

so soft — all the right letters into the teeny walkie-talkie.

Just like you practice.

And Sal will be counting on you! You, her only good

dog! You, her little mushki!

XXX.

Sally:

It was all so clear now. I was not going to cheat.

But how was I going to let Seemie know?

"Now, children," Mrs. Burke said as Señora Pangli left the room. "it's time for our first spelling bee."

I could simply NOT turn on the walkie-talkie.

But Seemie loved me so much, he might try to help me anyway — spelling the words really loudly.

Then I remembered that Seemie could read! (Duh!)

I scribbled the words in my notebook: "SEEMIE, I DON'T WANT TO CHEAT. SO DON'T SPELL ANY WORDS FOR ME."

I tore the note out as quietly as I could and put it in through the pack's unzipped opening. In order to give Seemie light, I tugged the pack into the aisle next to my desk and unzipped it a little more.

"Class," Ms. Burke said. "I've taken the liberty of dividing you into teams."

Seemie:

Oh no, it time!

And I got to warn Sally! I got to tell her I won't cross bridge, burn igloo!

I got to explain that it just not good for her!

Wait a second. What this?

"SEEMIE," it say. "I'M NOT GOING TO CHEAT. SO DON'T SPELL ANY WORDS FOR ME."

As I read the words, my bridge-not-crossing paws relax. It like I'm an esp. Alaskan Malamute after all.

But then, all sudden — YEOW! — something hit me. Something hard, sharp and ouch again and ouch again! Ouch! Ouch!

And we fall! YEOW! My whole body, whole pack!

Sally:

Yelps fire-engined through the classroom.

"Seemie! Are you okay?" I cried, running back to the pack. It had been knocked into the middle of the aisle and flipped over. A little white muzzle was falling out of the unzipped opening, a little white muzzle whimpering in pain.

"What IS that *thing*?" Raquelle cried, foot frozen mid-kick.

"What's that noise?" Ms. Burke said. Now, she too was next

to us. "Girls, whose pack is this?"

"It's mine," I whispered.

"And you *kicked* it?" she turned to Raquelle.

"She left it right in the middle of the floor," Raquelle whined.

I wanted to yell at her, 'I did not,' but I was too busy just trying to get to Seemie. He was still upside down/sideways/tangled all up in the backpack and the parts I could see looked terrified.

"But Sally, what's that little — Why, it looks like it's alive!"

"It's … my dog."

"Your dog?" Ms. Burke said. "Do you mean to tell me you've got a dog in that backpack? A live dog?"

She sounded so excited I was afraid she'd start to scream. Instead, she crouched next to me.

"Awww," she said, reaching out towards Seemie's muzzle. "Look at the poor little thing. Is his nose caught in that opening? My word, has he been in that pack all day?"

When I finally got the pack unzipped — my mom had used old-fashioned extra strong zippers — Seemie tumbled out in a mass of sweater and fur. I hugged him both as hard and gently as I could.

"Awww," Ms. Burke said again.

Then "*awww,*" said what sounded like every kid in the class.

"*Can I hold him?*"

"*No me.*"

"*Me first.*"

"*Me second!*"

As they crowded around, my note tumbled onto the floor, caught in a wrinkle of sweater —

"SEEMIE," I saw from the side, "I DON'T WANT —"

"What's that?" Raquelle said.

But before she could get down to it, Seemie half-slipped from my arms and scooped the note up, right onto his little pink tongue.

Oh, you little mushki!

Seemie:

Eeeuw.

A mouthful of paper is last thing I need. The only water I drunk all day just drops on good Sally's fingers.

Still, I (rrr-gulp) swallow.

"Is he choking?" Ms Burke cry.

"No, he's okay," Sally say. "It was just a little bit of doggy treat."

She don't have to go that far!

"Can I pat him?"

"Please!"

"Me, me!"

"Children, into your places, please." Ms. Burke say. "First, Sal, why don't you give him a little water. Here, use my cup."

Sally bring me water then as Ms. Burke put arm around me — she does smell like lavender. The water taste like coffee, but coffee way better than paper.

"Okay, Class, settle down. I don't know why Sally brought this little doggy to school," Ms. Burke say, "but we can't let him disturb our first spelling bee, can we? Is it okay if I hold him, Sally? I'm sure he'll be more

comfortable with me than in that bag."

"Yes, Ms. Burke," Sally whisper.

I swoop up in Ms. Burke's arms. She also smell like ...

chalk. (Which is not so good as cheese — still reminds me

of good old attic.)

"Team A, you go line up by that wall, and you Team B,

by the window."

XXXI.

Sally:

Now that the spelling bee was beginning, I wasn't so sure that I'd been right to call off the plan.

But if I was going to embarrass myself, I thought, at least I could do it without my ears hurting.

So, before going over to the Team B side of the room, I took off the walkie-talkie earring — the other one too, and slipped them inside one of the pockets of my backpack.

I gave one quick look at Seemie. He also seemed really nervous, though, in his case, it may have been because there were about twenty-five kids trying to grab him.

"Children, into positions please!" Ms. Burke said, holding Seemie carefully out of kid reach.

As everyone wandered to the sides of the room, I realized that a lot of them looked nervous too. Ritchie Parker was pulling on one side of his shirt so hard that a big piece of skin between his neck and shoulder showed. Hazel Kandel shut her eyes and recited something under her breath. (As I passed by, I heard "i before e except after c. I before e except after —") Olivia twisted one of her braids so tight, her finger was purple, and Raquelle was carrying a pencil in her mouth, one hand cupped over the side to try to hide her chewing.

"The first word is 'attempt.' 'Attempt.'" Ms. Burke said.

Roman Delavega, at the front of the Team A line, sighed, pushed his hair out of his eyes, began.

I wished so much I'd been first. I mean, I could spell 'attempt' without even trying.

The next word was "Genuine, Genuine."

Hazel spelled it with a J. Oh no! Team B gave one huge gasp, and Richie cried out, "Hazel!" But Ms. Burke glared so sharply at everyone, they all got quiet right away.

And suddenly it all just seemed silly. I mean, poor Hazel. Okay, so she misspelled a word. It wasn't a reason to get mad at her. I tried to send her a big smile.

"Lighthearted, lighthearted.

"Successful, successful."

"Special, special."

On and on, it went. Ms. Burke saying words (with Seemie up on her shoulder), kids saying letters.

I thought I had gotten calmer listening to everyone else; I thought I'd convinced myself it was all silly. But when it was actually my turn, my heart filled my throat so tightly, I could hardly speak. (Luckily, the word was one of Ruby's favorites — "automatic.")

Another round. More kids had to sit down but I got my next word right too — "celebrate."

Team B cheered me till Ms. Burke gave her hard look again. My cheeks were red, but in a good way. Seemie, looking down from Ms. Burke's shoulder, gave me a big dog grin.

Pradip turned out to be a wonderful speller, sometimes pronouncing the words in a funny Englishy-sounding way, but proceeding through all the letters just like that. People cheered him now too, and, though Richie and Estelle still called him "Dipster," they said it in a nice way: "yo, Dipster!"

I felt nervous every time it was my turn, but tried to just focus on the word (and not all the other kids).

Soon, there was hardly anyone left, just Pradip and me for Team B and Olivia and Sherelle for Team A. Then, I got "canine."

My heart sank. K and C's were something I had always had a

problem with.

I looked at Seemie, still in Ms. Burke's arms. I could feel him sending belief my way.

"Canine," I repeated slowly. "K," I tried.

Seemie's little head gave a small, firm, shake.

"I mean, 'C', I corrected quickly. Seemie nodded.

"Yes, that's it," I went on. "Canine. C-A-N-I-N-E."

"Exactly right," Ms. Burke said. The class — all the kids in Team B at least — cheered. This time Ms. Burke didn't glare at anyone.

Then, just as the kids grew quiet, "that's not fair!" Raquelle called out.

I froze.

"Because Sally would have know how to spell canine, right? After all, she's got a dog who can talk. Isn't that so, Sally?"

"Yeah," Gabby added. "Show us how he can talk, Sal."

XXXII.

Seemie:

Oh no!

Why did I shake my head? Why did I nod?

Oh no oh no oh no!

Sally:

"Come now, let's finish the spelling bee, Children," Ms. Burke said.

I could see Seemie trembling even from where I stood, the whites of his eyes showing all around their edges.

Even Ms. Burke noticed how scared he was. "I think the poor

dear misses you," she said, bringing him over to me.

I took him guiltily.

"Now, she'll probably talk to him," Raquelle sneered. "And I just bet that he'll talk back."

The rest of the class — Team A at least — laughed loudly. Even some of the kids in Team B laughed.

"Ssshhhh," I whispered to Seemie, as if I were just trying to comfort him.

The last word was "pantomime." I didn't even try it. (Honestly, I wouldn't even have been able to spell 'cat' just then.) But Pradip got it right away.

"That's wonderful, Pradip. Wonderful, Team B. You win this time, but both sides did a very good job. Now, just for the record, Pradip, do you know what the word 'pantomime' means?" Ms. Burke asked.

"'Pantomime,'" Pradip said slowly. "A pantomime is when people act things out silently, isn't it? That's also where the word 'mime' comes from. Except a mime is a person; a person who acts things out silently."

"That's it, exactly," Ms. Burke nodded.

Which suddenly gave me an idea.

Seemie:

It not regular scientists I don't like. I read about some really good ones in the back of the Dictionary. They have all names there. Newton who study gravity. Einstein with messy hair. Darwin who once had a beagle.

It just dog scientists I don't like.

They probably wouldn't like me either.

I try not to shiver. I try not to pant.

But it hard.

Sally:

"Is your little dog feeling better now, Sal?" Ms. Burke said, coming over to check on Seemie. "He's an awfully cute little thing."

"He is, Ms. Burke," I said, patting him. "He's really smart too."

"You've trained him?"

"Yes, ma'am. Would you like to see?"

"Of course. That is, if you don't think he'll be too unsettled by all the kids."

"No, he'll be okay. You'll be okay, won't you, Seemie, boy?"

Seemie looked at me fearfully. I gave him a scratch behind the ears. "It'll be okay, boy," I whispered.

"Yeah, come on, show us, Sal," Raquelle called out. "Show us how he can talk!"

"Okay, Seemie," I said, patting him. "We're just going to show them some of your *dog* tricks, all right?" I gave him a little wink. "You know all those tricks *dogs* do."

I put Seemie onto the floor.

"Okay, so, Seemie's not going to do anything that's um...rocket *science*. He's just going to do some *normal* everyday dog tricks. But it would help if there's *no talking*, okay?" I looked from the class to Seemie.

"You know, because Seemie needs to hear my commands," I added, turning my eyes back to the class. "So, if everyone could just *be quiet,* that would be great. Okay?"

I crouched down to Seemie. "You all set?"

It took a second. Then Seemie's muzzle broke out into that big old dog grin I loved so much, the lopsided one that showed all his teeth on one side.

"Sit, Seemie," I said.

He sat.

"Good boy." I patted him. (Oh, that fur felt good!)

"Give me a paw."

He gave me a paw.

"Now, shake — not that kind of shake —" (Seemie had started an all body shake.) "A hand — I mean, paw shake." Seemie stuck out his paw.

"Good boy. Now ... um ... beg, Seemie, beg," I said, gently waving my arms.

Seemie sat back on his haunches and waved his paws up and down. Little oohs and ahs broke out like fireflies lighting an evening field.

"Oh great," Raquelle groaned. "But I thought this was the dog that could *talk.*"

Seemie froze mid-beg.

But I was ready for this.

"Did I say he could talk, Raquelle? I meant that he could *speak*. Speak is the command people use when they want to get a dog to *bark*. So, *speak,* Seemie. *Speak!"*

Seemie grinned. Then, "rruff, ruff!" he barked.

"Sing, Seemie," I said. "Sing that song — um — 'Daisy!'"

Seemie broke into '**ruff**-ruff; **ruff**-ruff; ruff **ruff** ruff **ruff** ruff ruff' in a way that if you listened really really *really* hard sounded sort of like *The Bicycle Built for Two.*

"Oh my!" Ms. Burke said.

"Fabulous," Pradip crowed.

The class buzzed. Raquelle tried to look bored, but even her pouty face couldn't quite manage it.

"Play dead, Seemie."

Seemie (a much bigger ham than I'd ever imagined) thrust his front paws out to his sides, let out whimpering howl, and spun to the floor, twitching a minute or two before stretching silently onto his back.

The class gasped, then broke into applause.

Seemie
Playing Dead

Seemie playing dead.

Seemie playing dead

"I think that's enough for one day," I said, bending down to rub Seemie's tummy. He grinned from one side of his prone face, then, rolling over, curled up next to my feet.

"Incredible!" Ms. Burke burbled. "Absolutely amazing! Did you train him yourself, Sally?"

"Yes, ma'am."

"Well done! You must have an absolutely wonderful talent with animals, my dear."

I felt my cheeks reddening, but it was a good red.

"It wasn't so much, really. Seemie is an awfully smart dog," I said, patting him.

"Even so," Ms. Burke smiled. "You were the teacher."

XXXIII.

Seemie:

On the bus ride home, Sally pat me and whisper "oh, you little mushki," the whole way — that is, all the time she isn't rrr-fending off other kids who want to pat and whisper "oh, you little mushki." (I suddenly understand "mushki" too, even if it's not in Dictionary.)

As I sit there, being patted and whispered to, I realize being a little fuzzy dog's not so bad. No matter how I look in the mirr-rrr-ror.

When we get home, Sally officially apologize for

asking me to cheat, and I officially apologize for agreeing

to cheat. Then we go with Ruby for ice cream! And Sally

promise to get some flavor other than chocolate. Because

chocolate is bad for dogs, and I AM a dog!

XXXIV.

Sally:

To celebrate the fact that it was Friday and that I'd survived my first spelling bee, my mom and Seemie and I went to Scotto's ice cream stand.

Guess who was there!

Well, Raquelle for a little bit, with Gabby.

But I didn't let them bother me at all. I mean, when Raquelle started to say, "hey Gar —" I spoke right up.

"The name's Sally," I said. "Sally Marie Darma. And you know what? Those are my only names."

Then Seemie growled at her and she and Gabby hurried away to Raquelle's mom's car.

But Pradip was there too, with his mom. We sat on one of Scotto's benches even though it was getting cold, and, as we ate our ice cream, we laughed and talked and fed little bits (and sometimes big bits) to Seemie. (Seemie seemed to like Pradip a whole lot better by the way. Partly it was the ice cream, but mainly I think it was because Pradip was such a good speller.) Scotto, Ruby and Pradip's mom talked by Scotto's truck where a small heater was blowing.

Later that evening, I sat in my mom's workshop, patting Seemie's tummy every so often while Ruby worked on the Automatic Plantwaterer. She had dragged it back in from the kitchen because its accordion had torn loose.

"Maybe I should just junk the whole thing," she said, giving the Waterer her usual piercing fix-it look. Only this time, the look itself seemed kind of worn out.

"I mean," she sighed sadly, "maybe it's kind of a weird, big, drippy old thing even when it works just right."

A part of me wanted to shout, 'yes!' (As in 'yes, Mom, the plantwaterer IS a weird big drippy old thing.')

Then I thought of Raquelle's mom. She had been in the parking lot at Scotto's earlier, her hair still as stiff as a plastic helmet, her clothes, though this time blue and silver, still perfectly new, perfectly matching, her face still irritated.

As I looked back to Ruby, her hands carefully piecing together all the bits and pieces of old junk she'd saved for the good of the planet, a wave of happiness washed over me.

"Oh no, mom. You should fix the Plantwaterer. I mean, if it's not too much trouble."

"It's no trouble. At least not to me," she laughed.

"You know, Mom," I went on. "I've been experimenting with that backpack you made and it really is cool. I can carry it even if I put super heavy things in."

"That's the parachute silk," she smiled. "I'm so glad I finally found a good use for it."

"Me too."

Seemie turned over, eyes clouded with worry.

"Not that I'm planning to carry a lot of heavy stuff around in it," I added, giving him a quick pat.

And Seemie, shutting his eyes again, sighed.

"You little mushki," I whispered.

Seemie:

   Mmmmm....

ACKNOWLEDGEMENTS

Many thanks.

This book was so long in the making that those who helped in the early stages may not even remember. I do, though, and want especially to thank Marthe Jocelyn, Grace Cohen, Diana Barco, Alexandra Von Hoffman, Jeannie Hutchins, Rhona Saffer, and Alison Messina, who were kind enough to read and comment on early drafts; also thanks to my nephews Paul, John and Andrew Gustafson, who were kind enough to listen to early drafts, to my mother Phyllis Gustafson (who "always liked that doggy book") and my late father, Paul Gustafson, who always liked nearly everything I did.

Thanks to readers of my blog, http://Manicddaily.wordpress.com, especially Joy Ann Jones and Kerry O'Connor, who have allowed me to think of myself as an illustrator. Thanks also to Dr. Charles Robert Hayes and Robert C. Muffly.

Finally, my unlimited gratitude to my daughters, Meredith and Christina Martin, who both read and listened to early drafts (and to early and late kvetching), to Jason Martin, without whom I would have given up long ago, and to our dearest Pearl.

ABOUT THE AUTHOR

Karin Gustafson writes poetry, fiction and draws pictures, often of little dogs or elephants. She blogs (poetry mainly) as Manicddaily. She has previously written *1 Mississippi*, a children's counting book for lovers of watercolors and pachyderms (also illustrated by her); *Going on Somewhere*, a book of poetry illustrated by Diana Barco, cover by Jason Martin; *Nose Dive*, a comical young adult novel illustrated by Jonathan Segal, and *Nice*. Her poems are also included in *The dVerse Anthology: Voices of Contemporary World Poetry*, edited by Frank Watson.

BACKSTROKE BOOKS

213

Made in the USA
Charleston, SC
09 July 2016